Summer TO REMEMBER

MAIN STREET MINDEN
BOOK 4

Tara Grace Ericson

Tara Grace Ericson

To the wonderful people who
add color to my life.
Diversity is a beautiful thing
and I love you all.

Table of Contents

The 'Main Street Minden' Series

Falling on Main Street
Winter Wishes
Spring Fever
A Summer to Remember

Main Street Minden Novellas

Kissing in the Kitchen

Chapter 1

Danielle Washington threw the phone into the passenger seat and tapped her forehead on the steering wheel. She squeezed her eyes shut to hold back the tears stinging behind the shuttered lids. *Why is this happening to me?* First, some jerk broke into her apartment. They stole the only thing of value - her stand mixer and her personal cake decorating supplies. Now she was losing her job, too?

She didn't earn much money working at Cupcakes by Casey, not remotely enough to afford living in San Francisco, but she loved every minute. Her friend and boss, Casey, just called to tell her the store was closing. There was too much competition and they weren't earning enough to afford the lease.

Casey would continue baking special order cakes from her house, but there was no room for an employee in such a small business. Dani knew that even though it was devastating for her to hear, it was probably ten times harder for Casey. Not only was she taking a big step backwards on her dream bakery, but she had to fire a friend. As much as she knew she should feel bad for Casey, Dani was preoccupied with her own situation.

What am I supposed to do now? She didn't have a family. Danielle's parents had been nearly forty when she was born. Her mother died a few years ago and her father died when she was only eleven. Her mom's family had never been a part of her life, and her father's parents were gone, too. Danielle's only roommates were an artist even more broke than she was and her cat, Loki. Other than her friends, she was alone.

Dani took a deep breath and tried to compose herself. *There's no use in crying,* she thought. With a sniffle, she grabbed the keys from the cupholder and slipped them into the ignition. Turning the key resulted only in a *click, click, click* sound.

"You've got to be kidding me, God. Did I tick you off or something?" She threw a little tantrum, flailing around the seat as much as the small space would allow and stomping her feet on the floorboard. She looked up at the roof of the car and released the scream that had been building during weeks of frustration while she shook the steering wheel.

A car door slammed outside her window and she turned to see an old lady standing between their cars. Her eyes were wide and she slowly backed away from Danielle toward the rest of the parking lot.

Great. Now I scare little old ladies. Danielle couldn't help laughing at the poor woman's face. But the laughter soon turned to unrestrained sobs. *Is this going to be my life? An eighty-year struggle for money, acceptance, and happiness? And then I die.* Every time she thought she finally found her place, it was pulled out from under her. Culinary school had been her dream. Six months into the program, she'd had to quit her job working nights at the hotel. Which meant she ran out of money for school. The job at Casey's had been a godsend. She didn't have a degree, but Casey gave her a shot anyway. Danielle loved experimenting with new flavors and decorating cupcakes with seasonal designs. It was unlikely she could find another bakery to hire her for more than cleanup without her finished degree.

God, what am I going to do? I trust You; I swear I do. But seriously. I hope You aren't just messing with me.

I have a plan for you, a plan to prosper you and not to harm you.

She wiped her cheeks and took a few deep,

shuddering breaths. *Well, okay then. But can we get to the prospering part sooner rather than later?*

With one last sigh, Danielle grabbed her phone and keys and climbed out of the car. Now, she had to figure out how to get home. And how to get her car to the shop when it wouldn't start. And how to pay for the repairs. She glanced around and found the sign for the bus stop. Hopefully, her bus pass still had a few bucks on it. Otherwise she would have to resort to begging the driver to take pity on her. She officially had zero money in her account. Nothing to pay rent. Nothing to pay for the car.

With a glance skyward, she trudged toward the bus stop and spoke out loud. "Anytime now, God."

Dani felt the buzz in her palm and her phone lit up with an unfamiliar number. *Terre Haute, Indiana?* It sounded vaguely familiar, but Danielle definitely didn't know anyone there. She tried to picture Indiana on the map, but her geography was more than a bit rusty. With nothing better to do while she waited for the bus, she answered the phone.

"Hello?"

"Is this Beatrice Washington?"

Danielle rolled her eyes. She was still using her mother's cell phone number and telemarketers called all the time.

"This is her daughter. Beatrice died four years ago."

"Oh well, I didn't know that. Perhaps you can help me then? I'm calling on behalf of Margaret Woodson. Your aunt, I suppose. This is Ruth Coffman."

Danielle searched her memory and came up blank. "Who?"

"Beatrice's sister, Margaret."

"Aunt Maggie?" The name sounded familiar, but Danielle couldn't remember her aunt. Had she ever met her? While Dani was young, her mother hadn't mentioned her family much. When Danielle asked, her mother always avoided the topic.

"I'm sorry to tell you that your aunt is in the hospital. Your mom is listed as the emergency contact."

Confused, Danielle responded, "Okay? What am I supposed to do about it?"

The woman on the phone let out a huff. "She's going to be okay, thanks for asking." Danielle felt a tinge of guilt before the woman continued. "Look, Margaret broke her hip and needs someone to stay with her for a while and help run her bakery."

Danielle sat up straight on the bus stop bench. "Bakery?" With one word, this call was much more interesting.

"I don't know if she has any other family. She doesn't even know I'm making this call. But she needs her family. And I guess that's you."

"Where exactly do I need to go?" Danielle tried

to sound more friendly and disguise the fact she had no idea where her aunt lived.

"She's at the hospital in Greencastle."

"Indiana?" Danielle ventured a guess and crossed her fingers she didn't sound completely ignorant.

"Of course. When can you get here?"

Danielle considered her options. There was nothing for her here anymore. She wasn't sure how she would get to Indiana, but surely she had a credit card that wasn't quite maxed out and could charge the airfare.

"I'll head that way as soon as I can. It may take a few days."

"That's okay, Sweetie. She'll be in the hospital for at least a week and at the rehab center for a couple weeks after that. You just call me when you are in town and I'll help you get settled at her house."

Huh, Danielle thought, *that's an interesting turn of events. I'm moving to Indiana.* She hadn't realized Aunt Maggie was still around or that she owned a bakery. A vague memory of standing on a chair mixing a cake with her aunt surfaced. Was that where she got her love of baking? It wasn't from her mother, that was for sure.

The bus pulled into the loading zone and she gathered her things. Time to go pick up Loki and let Willow, the starving artist, know she was on her own for the rent from here on out. *Indiana, here we come.*

*****

She went online and booked a flight for the next day. Then, she called her friend and former boss, Casey, to tell her about the change in life plans. Only thirty minutes had passed since Casey told her about the store closing.

"Hey Case."

"Hey, Danielle. Are you doing alright? You know I really am sorry I couldn't keep you on at the shop, right?"

"Yeah, I know. It's not your fault."

"It's not your fault either, and I'll give you a great recommendation wherever you end up next."

She felt a lump in her throat at her best friend's kindness. "Thanks, Casey. Actually, about that... I wanted to let you know I am moving to Indiana."

"Indiana? Are you sure this isn't a knee-jerk reaction?"

"Yeah," Danielle said with a laugh. "Who would have thought? But apparently, I have an aunt there and she needs some help. And you'll never guess what else!"

"What?"

"She owns a bakery there!" Dani couldn't hide her excitement.

"Wow. That's amazing."

"I thought so too. It was like this flashing neon sign from God saying 'Go this way'."

"That's great, Danielle. I hope it works out. When do you leave?"

"I leave tomorrow," she admitted.

"Wow! So soon!" Casey's enthusiasm did little to hide her surprise.

"Yeah, Aunt Maggie broke her hip and is still in the hospital. Plus, my car broke down and there really isn't much reason to stay." Dani tried to force any self-pity out of her voice. It was fact and not worth moaning over any more.

"Aw, man. I'm sorry. Well, tonight you should come to Knit Night and hang out with all of us. Besides, I wanted to see the final version of the dragon amigurumi you almost had done last time."

Dani grinned. "That sounds great. I forgot all about Knit Night. And he was a Charizard." Not that the name of the dragon-type Pokémon would mean much to Casey.

"Whatever. He was cute. So, you'll come tonight?

'Yep. I'll be there."

It didn't take long for Danielle to pack her things. She didn't have much. Other than her clothes for tomorrow and the few things Loki would need, she threw her things in a suitcase. Willow was painting in her room with the music up loud. She gave a distracted acknowledgment when Danielle tried to explain that she was leaving the next day and not planning to come back. Danielle wasn't sure if the girl realized she was now on her own for rent again, but shrugged it off. She'd done her best. Willow was an interesting one. They'd lived together for almost six months, but only had a handful of conversations. Willow almost always wore black, and dyed her hair various colors depending on her mood. This month, it was silvery-gray with purple on the ends. She hardly spent any time outside, and her ghost-white skin was so delicate it was nearly see-through.

Danielle couldn't imagine doing something like that to her hair. It was thick and coarse; the bleach and color wouldn't do it any favors. Not to mention how odd she thought it would look with her naturally dark skin - the result of her pale Midwestern mother falling in love with a black man; Dani's father. Her mom, Beatrice had come to California to be an actress, much to her parents' chagrin. Then, according to her mom, they had cut off all ties when she had married someone they didn't approve of.

What was she doing, deciding to go to Indiana? If her mother's parents had disowned Beatrice for marrying her father, what would her sister think of her mixed-race niece showing up unannounced? Maybe the thought of running the bakery was blinding her. This had to be a bad decision.

God, are you sure?

She didn't receive an answer, except in a flood of released tension through her body. *Okay. I can do this.*

She had her memory of Aunt Maggie, and even though it wasn't a vivid memory - it wasn't a negative one either. Her aunt had laughed with her and played with her. Surely, she wasn't a villain! Could there be more to the story than her mother had shared? Why had they never gone to visit? Her Nana and Pops on her dad's side had been the only grandparents she'd ever known. They were wonderful people and she loved nothing more than helping Pops fix the car or playing card games with Nana.

Her Dad had been nearly forty when she was born, her mom in her mid-thirties, so Nana and Pops had always seemed ancient to her. When her mom died four years ago, she was the last person Danielle really had. Dad died when she was eleven, the victim of a drunk driver. Nana and Pops had been gone since she was in high school. Suddenly, Danielle was alone except for friends. If there was even a small chance she could recover some lost family connection back in Indiana, she had to try. For all she knew, she had cousins! Worst-case scenario, she ran the bakery and could use that experience to land a job down the road. She was praying for something better than the worst case, though.

Knit Night happened twice a month at Adele's apartment. The group typically included Adele Watson, who worked as the assistant to some big shot CEO here in San Francisco, Emily, Liz, and Casey. There were others who came occasionally, but those four were the cornerstone. Adele even let the group meet at her apartment when she had to travel for work. Apparently, her boss was super demanding but Adele loved working for him.

Danielle grabbed her crochet bag and the finished Charizard to show Casey. Her current work in progress was a little Yoda. He even wore a little Jedi robe. It made her smile every time she saw it. "Finish you, I will," she said to the half-finished character in her best Yoda impersonation.

Chapter 2

Mark could feel the impatience, thick in the air of his classroom as he flipped to another slide on the PowerPoint. There was one week left of school before summer vacation arrived.

"The final is on Thursday, guys. We've got to review today so you can prepare for the test." Mark saw Amber's hand shoot up, her fingertips wiggling as they reached to the ceiling. He nodded at her.

"What are we doing tomorrow and Wednesday?"

Like most experienced teachers, Mark was well aware of the time warp that encompassed every school, slowing down the passage of time exponentially as they moved closer to the end. Students felt it too. Disappointment filled their faces each day they slumped into their seats and realized the agenda wasn't an end-of-the-year movie.

Teaching social studies to middle schoolers didn't seem like a dream job to most people, but he loved it. Students in middle school were obnoxious and relentlessly weird. They were just figuring out who they were, growing out of friendships that had persevered since kindergarten and exploring their own interests. For some, it was video games. For others, it was books or music. Some found joy in athletics. Admittedly, those were the ones Mark struggled to connect with the most. No doubt his brother, Daniel would understand them.

"I'm not telling. But I'd recommend you all start studying tonight so you don't let your teammates down." He made eye contact with a few of the students he knew procrastinated. To generate interest, he revealed the prize, "There might be ice cream on the line."

Whispers spread through the room as students speculated. He let them chatter for a few moments before raising both arms, the laptop remote in one hand. "Okay, okay. Bring it down a notch. You won't know what to study if we don't make it through this before the bell rings."

The teaser about tomorrow's activities worked and the class took notes with renewed interest. He would dangle the mystery to all his classes, three periods of sixth graders and three periods of seventh graders. Designing the test review for every unit was especially fun for him. So far this year, they had played Team Jeopardy, Who Wants to be a Millionaire, and a version of the classic board game Sorry! Students had really enjoyed being able to sabotage the other teams and knock their pieces back to home base.

His plan for tomorrow was his favorite yet. The teasing he'd endured from his brothers when he dabbled in the well-known role-playing game, Quest, nearly caused him to give it up entirely, but he couldn't help but love the creative problem-solving the game involved. For the next two days, his classes would role-play their way through the world of his creation while answering questions based on the material they covered in class all year. He would act as the "Journey Master". His inner geek was excited.

He made it through the last slides and answered a few more questions from his class. The bell rang, signaling the end of the period. "Don't forget, your final projects are due tomorrow!" Binders slammed shut and zippers buzzed as the class packed up their books and pencil cases before heading toward the hallway.

Five more classes to go today, plus lunchroom duty and his free period. He would use the free period to touch up the game. His student aid, Brittany, could grade the worksheets he collected today.

He felt his phone vibrate and pulled it out of his pocket, seeing Luke Brand's name on the text notification.

LB: When can you
start again?

For the past five years, Mark worked part-time during the summers for Luke's landscaping company, mowing lawns and trimming bushes. It kept him busy and while he loved teaching, the salary wasn't exactly generous. Plus, he hated sports and working out, so the manual labor was the only fitness regimen he stuck to. Classes ended this Friday; Mark knew he would have grades to enter and would need to clean up his classroom Monday and Tuesday.

MD: I'll probably start
Wednesday if that's
cool?

LB: Sounds good.
See you then.

He would enjoy spending time outside. He knew he looked pale during the winter months. Too much time playing video games and creating test review activities. Students for his next class started filing into the classroom and finding their seats. Seats weren't assigned, but by a few weeks into the school year, everyone generally gravitated to the same seat each day.

His pulse started to pick up and he double-checked the slideshow and projector were working. He hated the few times he had been unprepared when the bell rang to signal the start of class. It made him feel like a terrible teacher, though he was sure most of the student never noticed.

He watched the interactions of the students as he waited for the bell. David was well-liked by his classmates and he joked with Stephanie in the next seat, making her blush. Chloe sat quietly in the back row, immersed in a novel. She would begrudgingly put it away after the bell rang. If class was interesting, it would stay in her bag. If she got bored, he would see her sneak it out and read under her desk. She was smart and her grade wouldn't suffer. He still hoped every day that he could keep her engaged, just like every other student.

Amused, he watched Morgan pass a note to her friend Kayleigh and saw Carter tap Trevor on the one shoulder before ducking around the other. Carter laughed loudly when Trevor turned to find no one there and Mark tried to hide his smile when Trevor pretended to throw his pencil at his friend. He surveyed the room, looking for anyone withdrawn or upset. Teaching middle schoolers was less about curriculum and more about relationships. He knew students were more likely to put effort into a class if they liked the teacher and didn't want to disappoint them. He wasn't easy on them, but he tried to be funny and genuine. Encouraging each student to show him what they could do and giving them opportunities to surprise him with their creativity made his job more fun.

Mark loved encouraging his students to be themselves. He remembered his own awkward pre-teen years and cringed. His favorite teacher at the time was Mr. Wragge. Having a male teacher had been a novelty. And judging by the ratio of men in his pool of co-workers, it hadn't changed much over the years. He hoped he was an example to the adolescent boys at the school that it was okay to be smart and to not follow the crowd. Embracing his quirkiness was the only way Mark knew to navigate life.

His favorite project each year was the semester-long assignment he gave each class. They had almost complete freedom to decide the topic and the type of project. Each year, he received countless posters about historical figures or basic research papers covering a specific culture. But the best were surprises. A girl last year wrote an entire ten-thousand-word short story of a Jewish child during the holocaust. A quirky young man created an extensive board game based on Alexander the

Great's conquests. Last semester, his favorite was a three by five-foot canvas painting of the Amazon rain forest. The artist researched different plants and animals present in the rain forest and included dozens of them in the painting. Giving his students the freedom to tie their interests and strengths into his class resulted in amazing projects. Plus, the students had pride in their projects that wouldn't happen if he assigned something of his own design.

The bell rang and Mark strolled to the front of the classroom. "Alright, alright. Everybody, settle down. I'm going to walk through the topics that will be covered on Friday's final. Your semester projects are due tomorrow! Don't forget to bring it in. It's worth fifteen percent of your grade for the semester. And if you haven't started it yet?" Mark raised an eyebrow and scanned the length of the room. "You've made a very poor life decision and I feel no sympathy for you." Chuckles from the class were scattered. He'd been saying the same line every week since January.

"Any questions?" Ignoring the hands that went up, he continued, "Good. Here we go." Then he sighed heavily and pointed to David. "Ugh, fine, what?" He pretended to be exasperated but broke character and laughed.

David smiled and asked, "Are we going to get our projects back?"

Mark replied. "Yes. I will give them back on

Friday. I may ask to keep a few good examples of the kinds of projects I look for, but you don't have to say yes. Anything else? Okay, let's get started." He flipped on the projector and leaned on an empty desk in the third row. "I'd write this down if I were you."

*****

When Dani arrived at Knit Night, she knocked and waited. No one answered but she heard the laughter inside the apartment and opened the door to stick her head in.

"I'm a crocheter, but I come in peace!"

"Danielle!" The chorus of voices rose from the seating area in the living room, and she turned the corner to see Casey, Emily, and Liz. Casey's knitting needles were clicking as she quickly knit another row on what appeared to be a scarf. There wasn't even a pause as she greeted Danielle.

Liz and Emily were currently snacking and chatting instead of knitting. Emily had gorgeous creamy skin and almond-shaped eyes, framed in glasses she switched out regularly with different colors and types. Liz was a stark contrast. She had the most gorgeous red hair and pale skin dotted with freckles. She towered over Emily, even seated on the couch. Emily worked at the local zoo as a veterinarian. Liz worked in design and engineering for Dawson Dynamics, the tech company responsible for apps of all kinds. Danielle eyed the snack mix. The realization that she hadn't eaten all day suddenly made her aware of the angry emptiness in her stomach.

Adele entered from the kitchen across the room, her slightly plump frame still balanced on strappy high heels from her day at work. She was carrying a plate of cheese, meat and crackers and a small metal bucket filled with wrapped Dove chocolates. 'The Chocolate Bucket' was a sacred Knit Night tradition, passed around as the women told tales of their current love woes, work challenges, and family drama.

Everything seemed a little better when there was chocolate in your hand. At least, that's what Danielle remembered Adele saying. Thanking God for the small blessing of daily bread in the form of cheese and crackers, she greeted everyone and took the seat next to Casey.

Casey put down her knitting and gave Danielle a quick hug. "I'm so glad you came, Dani. I can't believe you are moving!"

Emily spoke up from across the room. "You're moving?"

Danielle nodded. "Yeah, I'm flying to Indiana tomorrow."

"Wow!" It was Adele's turn to chime in. "What is in Indiana?"

Danielle reached for some cheese and took a bite. "I don't really know, honestly. My aunt, who I haven't seen since I was like, six years old, needs some help. And well, there really isn't much reason for me to stay here anymore."

"What do you mean? What about Casey and the bakery?" Emily asked.

Danielle turned to Casey. "You haven't told them yet?"

Casey sighed. "No. I guess I'm still hoping something will help." She looked around and explained to the group, "I have to close the store. There just isn't enough business to cover the lease. Most of my business comes from scheduled events anyway, and I can do those out of my house. So, I had to let Danielle go." She winced at the admission.

"Oh man, that totally sucks."

"Yeah, I'm sorry Casey. I know you worked really hard to make the store work." Adele poured a glass of wine for Casey and handed it to her.

Accepting the drink, Casey sniffed. "It's okay. I'm not giving up. This is just a little setback. I still have tons of loyal customers and cakes booked for the next six months." She took a sip and then looked back at Danielle. "I'm just sorry it means that Dani is leaving town."

Danielle shook her head. "It's really okay, Case. God has really given me a good feeling about this. I think I'm supposed to go. Besides, I'll come back to visit! I promise."

"You better. There is always a spot for you at the circle. And a chocolate!" Adele had her priorities, that was sure. She took a chocolate out of the bucket and passed it around. When she unwrapped her chocolate, she read the saying from the inside of the wrapper. "Ignite your sense of adventure." She looked up. "I think I got Danielle's. You're the one going on an adventure!"

Danielle smiled and grabbed her own chocolate. Unwrapping it, she read it and her lips lifted. "No. I'm pretty sure I got mine. *Things have to fall apart for them to fall together.*" She gave a half-hearted chuckle. "Things certainly fell apart here. No job, no money. Did I mention that my car broke down? I think things will come together in Indiana. I'm just a little terrified that my aunt will be mad I'm there. I don't think she knows I'm coming. And things didn't exactly end well with my mom and her family." She briefly explained the situation that led to her mom being unwelcome in Indiana and living in California.

"Well, I hope she has an open mind. But remember, you don't need anyone there to accept you. God has already adopted you and called you His own. Dani, maybe we could pray for you before you leave?" Casey offered and the others murmured their agreement.

Danielle was touched and the lump in her throat prevented her from speaking. So, she simply nodded. Would she find friends like this in Indiana? Could she find friends that would pray over her without reservation and cover her in love and laughter?

Adele walked over and stood behind Danielle on the couch. Emily and Liz stood around the side and front, and her friends surrounded her. Casey grabbed her hand and started to pray. By the end, there were tears running down Danielle's cheeks and she grabbed a napkin to wipe her nose.

"Aw, thanks guys. I'm going to miss you something fierce."

"We know," Adele joked, "but it's going to be awesome."

"Okay, now enough with the sappy stuff. Show me that dragon you made. I'm so impressed with all your 3-D characters. Crochet is so cool that you can do stuffed animals!"

The rest of the night was filled with laughter and yarn and food and chocolate. Knit Night was something special. Hopping on the bus toward her apartment for one last night, she said a quick prayer of thanks for the women there and a plea for a support system in Indiana. She had a feeling she would need it.

Chapter 3

The rest of the week flew by. Between the review game, grading the final projects, and giving and grading the final exam; he was exhausted. His students, with few exceptions, had done amazing work on their projects. Brittany's final project had surprised him, though. As his aide, he knew she was an excellent student. But her project was low-effort and her grade reflected it.

After receiving the C on the project and taking the test on Friday, she hadn't even shown up for her Student Aide period. Technically, that was skipping class, but he wouldn't report it. She was a good kid. Probably just overwhelmed by the end of the school year. It hurt her final grade though. When he tallied on Monday, she had fallen from a solid A to a low B.

He clicked his tongue and grabbed the next final. Red pen in hand, he began reading the answer to the first essay. The hallways and classrooms stood impossibly empty on these days, when only the teachers and staff wandered the halls. Footsteps echoed outside his classroom and stopped by his open door.

When he glanced up, he saw Virgie Ada, the music teacher. The older woman had been teaching for nearly fifty years and could have retired ages ago. Virgie's energy at over seventy was inspiring, and Mark loved his talks with the kind teacher. She was sturdy and vibrant, healthier at her age than many people he knew in their fifties.

"Hello, Mark. How's it going today?"

He leaned back in his office chair. "Not bad. Only about fifty more finals to grade and enter. How are you, Mrs. Ada?"

She waved a hand. "Just going for a little walk. My work is easy. Music is pass/fail. If the kids show up and pretend to pay attention, I can give them a passing grade." She shrugged with a laugh.

"Must be nice!"

"It is, and it isn't. It's hard to make them care. If they don't love music or think they have 'talent', they mostly just endure the class." She shook her head in disappointment.

Mark considered her statement. "Hmmm, that would be hard. And you still have in-service days?"

"Yep. No exceptions." She rolled her eyes.

Mark stood up and leaned on his desk. "When kids don't like your class, does it make you feel like a bad teacher?"

Virgie tilted her head in thought. "Sometimes, I guess. Especially when I was younger. But I have the other students who reassure me. The students who tell me they never had rhythm. Or that they didn't enjoy 'old people music' before I introduced them to jazz. Why do you ask?"

"I don't know. I guess when the grades are in and each student's experience becomes a number and a letter, I wonder how I did. If I made a difference."

"You did. You know that, right?" She leaned against the door frame, her pastel blouse wrinkling against the metal. "I hear kids talking about your class all the time before the bell rings. They love you. They couldn't stop gushing about the Dynasties and Dragons game you played last week. I even heard Tucker Phillips correcting someone on the five pillars of Islam." She raised an eyebrow and Mark laughed.

"Well, that's a surprise. He doesn't really participate in class."

"Exactly. Ask any other teacher in this school and they'd pronounce him dumb as a rock. But in your class? He pays attention. What was his final grade?"

Mark tried to remember. "B minus, I think?" It hadn't seemed that significant. Tucker had done a decent job all year, after a bit of a rocky start. He was quiet in class, but turned in homework and did okay on tests.

"I don't think he got above a C in anything else. You make a difference. Don't let anything or anyone tell you differently. Plus, if you stick around long enough - these kids will keep you young." She said the last part with a wink and he laughed. *So that was her secret fountain of youth*, he mused.

"Thanks, Virgie. I appreciate it. So do you. Music is crazy important, even to those of us who can't carry a tune in a backpack."

She smiled. "Thanks, Mark. I think so, too."

"I better get back to these tests."

"Sure, I better get back to... well, organizing the instrument room, I suppose."

Mark considered what she'd said. His brothers gave him a hard time when he became a teacher. To his NFL-bound brother, it was girly and unimpressive. To Malachi, always attached to his computer, it was a waste of time. Malachi had created dozens of best-selling smartphone apps as the CEO of Dawson Dynamics.

The only one of his brothers who understood was Stephen. He was a youth pastor in Terre Haute and they were both passionate about the next generation, albeit in different ways.

Mark's mom supported all her children, no matter what they decided. Gideon graduated a few weeks ago with a degree in Journalism and didn't have a job lined up yet. In Mark's opinion, their parents coddled him. Living in his parents' basement sounded awful to him, but then Mark had always been independent. He'd take his small house in Minden any day. Visits home were wonderful and stressful. She tried to feed him like he was the NFL defensive linebacker and hounded him about finding a wife and giving her grandbabies. Despite having five boys, the oldest nearing forty years old, none had given her a daughter-in-law or grandkids yet.

As much as he loved his brothers, he always felt like an outsider. Stephen played guitar, and Gideon read a lot, but none of them were "geeky" like he was in high school. It turned out Mark's love of superheroes and fantasy books wasn't exactly the popular thing. Thanks to recent movies, his collection of original Spiderman comic books was now considered "Awesome!" by the jocks in his classes.

In high school, he would rather spend his lunch hour reading them than goofing around with friends. Some of his best friends he'd never met in real life. In college, he'd grown more comfortable in his skin and embraced his interests. He'd spent a lot of time learning to accept himself for the person he was.

But it was still hard not to be envious of Daniel's natural athletic ability or Malachi's acute business sense and knack for innovation. In the shadow of incredibly high-achieving siblings, it was easy to feel overlooked.

It would devastate his mother to know he felt that way. He knew both his parents loved him and gave as much value to his work as that of his brothers. Here in Minden, he found a community. His best friends were Luke Brand and Todd Flynn. Luke owned the landscaping company and Todd went to school with him and remained in Minden after graduation. Right now, they were both in newlywed bliss. First Luke, then Todd and Chrissy. Why was it so hard to find love? If only he and Mandy had more in common. But he couldn't imagine playing video games with her or watching the newest Star Trek movie. Luke told him it was unrealistic to dream he could find a woman who was beautiful, smart, and understood the world of Middle Earth. Why was it crazy to want a best friend and partner all in one?

*****

Mark studied the exterior of his parent's home, the one he'd grown up in. It could use a fresh coat of paint, and the grass was two inches too long. Dandelions sprung up between the cracks of the sidewalk. He kept telling his Dad to hire someone, but he was stubborn. Maybe Mark could convince Luke to let him mow it as part of his route. His dad might not be so reluctant if it was Mark doing the work. The house could definitely use some updates. He knew Daniel had offered to buy them a new house when he got his first big contract in the NFL, but his parents insisted they would be happier here. Daniel hadn't visited for months, but Mark decided to call him and hint that someone should spring for renovations.

He opened the door and inhaled the garlicky smell of mom's homemade spaghetti sauce. Gravy, she called it. He removed his shoes, placing them in the basket under the bench. No shoes in the house was one of the non-negotiable rules his mother held for the past forty years. The house had never been perfectly clean; there were always puzzles, Lego, and Nerf gun darts littering the floor of any given room. But shoes came off and the action was automatic even a dozen years after moving out. "Hey, Mom," he said as he turned the corner into the kitchen. His mother was full-blooded Italian, but she'd lived here all her life. Apparently, he still had family in Italy, but he'd never met them. Mom special-ordered from Fratello Chocolate Company which she proudly claimed was owned by her cousin.

"Marco!" His mom hurried around the counter

and opened her arms to embrace him. "How is my favorite son?" Every one of her sons was Donna Dawson's favorite, according to her. The running joke warmed his heart. As easy as it was to feel overshadowed by his brothers, Mom and Dad never failed to give every son their full attention.

Gideon walked around the corner, book in hand. "Hey, Mark."

Mark embraced his brother and slapped him on the back. "Gideon. Congratulations on graduating, bud! Sorry I couldn't make it for the ceremony."

"Eh, don't be. It was five hours long and excruciatingly boring. Right, Mom?"

"Of course, it wasn't boring, sweetheart." She waited until Gideon turned away and then made eye contact with Mark. She nodded and mouthed "Super boring."

Mark coughed to cover a laugh and Gideon gave his mom a glare. "I saw that."

"I'm sorry, honey. We loved watching you graduate. It was the other three thousand people we didn't want to watch."

Mark spoke up, "Well, either way - you did it! What are you going to do now?"

Gideon shrugged. "I don't know. I'm looking for jobs, but nothing feels right."

Mark fought the urge to roll his eyes at his younger brother. Gideon had been the unexpected child, born when Mark was seven. Gideon was the baby and the typical youngest sibling. Mark just shook his head in response and said, "You'll find something."

His dad walked in the room and his booming voice filled the small space. "Markie!"

"Hey Dad. I thought you agreed to stop calling me that! I'm twenty-nine years old for crying out loud." Was it too much to ask to lose the nickname Daniel had given him when Mark was a toddler?

"Bah." His dad waved a hand and then laid it heavily on Mark's shoulder. Richard Dawson was a big guy - six and a half feet tall and built like a linebacker. Three of his sons inherited those genes, but Mark must have missed out. Oh, he was tall enough, but Mark couldn't seem to build muscle, no matter how he tried. Malachi and Gideon were big and muscular like their father. It was a nice change when Gideon was born. He finally had a size advantage, at least when Gideon was young.

"Is Stephen coming tonight?" he asked.

His mother shook her head. "No, he's giving the sermon for church next week and wanted the extra time to prep."

"Cool. Are you going?" Though he and his parents still attended the local Baptist church, sometimes when Stephen was preaching, they made the drive to Terre Haute and the large church where he worked.

"Oh yes. We just love to hear him share the

Word."

"Cool. Count me in. I'll sit in the front row to make faces at him." His mom gave him a light whack on the back of the head.

"You will do no such thing, Mark Anthony Dawson."

He hung his head, pretending to be ashamed. "Yes, ma'am." *It's good to be home.*

Chapter 4

After landing in Indianapolis, Danielle searched
for the person Miss Ruth promised to send to pick
her up. Danielle had called her last night to ask for
the address, and the kind older woman insisted on
sending her son-in-law. Seeing as she really didn't
want to spend the money on an hour-long cab ride,
she agreed. She scanned the atrium for a stranger
and wished she had another option. For several
minutes, she stood alone, glancing around the space
every few moments hoping someone would stick
out.

Dani spotted a man, suntanned and dressed in
worn jeans and a green polo. He was looking down
the corridor, waiting for someone. He had a small
piece of paper with something written in pen. The

letters weren't dark enough for her to read, though. She inched closer, trying not to draw his attention. What did it say?

He must have noticed her eying his poor excuse for a sign, because he looked at her and said, "Oh, shoot. Are you Danielle?"

She just nodded and his face broke into a relieved smile. He glanced at his wrinkled paper and then crumpled it up. "I guess this wasn't doing a great job. I didn't have much in my truck for a sign when I thought about it." He stuck out his hand. "I'm Luke, by the way."

"Danielle."

"Welcome to Indiana, Danielle. Here, let me grab that and we can head to my truck." He grabbed the suitcase sitting beside her and she held Loki's small carrier and followed him. On their walk toward the parking garage, Luke gave an embarrassed confession. "I'm sorry I didn't get your attention sooner. You weren't exactly what I was expecting."

She frowned. What did that mean? She had tried to dress up a bit and wear something other than the printed t-shirts with sarcastic sayings and comic book heroes she typically favored.

"Ruth told me you were Margaret's niece and well, to be frank, she didn't tell me you were..." He trailed off.

Oh. Here we go. "Black?" she supplied. *I guess*

I'm not in California anymore.

"Well, yeah. I'm sorry, it just caught me off guard. All these years and Margaret never mentioned..."

"Maybe she forgot." Internally, Danielle winced at the bitter tone of her voice. True, it had been more than twenty years since she had seen her aunt, but she had no idea what to expect. She sent a quick prayer to heaven. *Soften my heart, Father.* She saw the panic in Luke's eyes. "I'm sorry. It's been a long day already and I'm crabby. It's not a big deal. We found each other and I'm guessing the reason Ruth didn't mention it is she didn't know. I still don't think Aunt Maggie knows I'm coming."

"I'm sure she will be thrilled, Danielle. Ruth said Margaret's been real blue since she fell. Plus, Main Street just isn't the same without the scent of fresh-baked cookies from The Rolling Pin"

That got Danielle's attention, and they spent the drive talking about the bakery and the small town of Minden. Danielle learned Luke had moved there when he married Rachel, Ruth's daughter and when Rachel had died, he had stayed. Luke invited her over for dinner to meet Charlotte, his new wife. "Oh, you'll love Charlotte. She's from the city, just like you. I'm sure you can commiserate over the lack of shopping or something."

"Or something," she agreed. Danielle wasn't exactly a big shopper. Unless it was for yarn. Or comic books. But it would be nice to have a friend. Luke was certainly nice enough. There was something welcoming about him. Plus, he had Christian music on quietly in the background during their drive and she caught him humming along when the conversation slowed. She could connect with Charlotte and keep her more geeky tendencies under wraps. No point in sharing with the entire town just how different she was. Skin color was one thing; she'd already figured the small Indiana town would be pretty homogeneous. But her unique interests would only add to the scrutiny. Nope, it was better if she was normal.

Luke took her to Ruth's and Danielle immediately adored the older woman. Her red hair and colorful outfit made a statement about the kind of woman Ruth was. Plus, as she watched Ruth's eyes, she saw no hesitation or hint of surprise at Danielle's appearance. She simply wrapped her in a hug and whispered, "Oh, I'm so glad you are finally here. Call me Miss Ruth; everyone else does."

Finally? It's only been three days. She nodded, "So am I."

Luke said goodbye and kissed Ruth on the cheek. Miss Ruth offered her food, and though it was the middle of the afternoon in Minden, Danielle realized it was nearly lunch in California and she was starving. Ruth lit up when she accepted her offer for a snack and expressed how much she loved

feeding people. Danielle watched her buzz around
the kitchen and listened to her talk about Minden
and Luke and Charlotte. She mentioned Norm, her
boyfriend, with a blush as she sliced a cucumber.
Danielle couldn't help but smile at the shy way the
older woman spoke of him, smoothing her fiery red
hair as though he might walk in any moment.

After her snack, Miss Ruth took her to
Margaret's home and let her in to drop off her
things. The small house was clean and smelled like
cinnamon pot-pourri. Inhaling the spicy air, her
eyes filled with tears. Beatrice preferred cinnamon
as well, burning holiday candles all year long.
Margaret's house smelled like home and Dani
exhaled, feeling the tension of the trip and the stress
of the mess she'd left in California melt away. *Oh,
God. You've got this, don't you? Sorry for doubting
you.*

Danielle dropped her bags and settled Loki with
water, food, and a litter box. They didn't linger at
Margaret's house, but instead, Ruth took her to the
rehab center.

"Does she know I'm coming?"

Miss Ruth pressed her lips together. "Well... No.
She doesn't."

"Miss Ruth! What if she doesn't want me here? I
can't exactly afford to go back. It's been twenty
years since I saw my aunt."

"I know, dear. Just trust me. Trust *God,*" Ruth

pleaded with her.

Danielle sighed. "Okay. I can do this." She looked at Ruth pointedly. "But if she's mad at anyone, it better be you."

Ruth nodded. "That's fair. I can take it."

Outside Margaret's room, Danielle rolled her shoulders back and took a deep breath for courage. She tapped on the doorframe and walked in. In the bed along the back wall, she recognized her aunt. Features so similar to her own mother made her do a double take. Compared to her last memories of Maggie in California, this woman was a stranger. The rich, brown hair of her memory was replaced with a silvery-gray, cut short in a modern pixie. *Whoa. Not so traditional, are we Aunt Maggie?*

Margaret's eyes met hers and recognition flickered. "Dani? Is that you?" She looked back and forth between Danielle and Ruth and a wide smile filled her face. "Ruth, what did you do?"

Ruth made her way across the room and sat on the edge of the bed beside her friend. "I'm sorry I didn't tell you sooner. You would've tried to convince me not to call. And the truth is - Danielle needs to be here. For herself as much as for you."

Danielle didn't know how Ruth knew, but she figured it was true. She would be in San Francisco if she still had a job. Or if God hadn't made it so obvious she needed to come. In that case, she would probably be trying to find a waitressing job to cover next month's rent.

"Hey, Aunt Maggie."

Margaret laughed. "Oh, child. It is so good to hear those words again. I've missed you so much."

"You have?" Dani reached up to rub her neck. *If she missed me, where has she been all this time?* Margaret smiled and nodded slowly against her pillow. Her pale skin hung loose on her cheekbones and she closed her eyes for a moment before opening them again. "You're exhausted. We'll come back later and we can talk."

Margaret just nodded again; her eyes already closed. Ruth and Danielle walked quietly out of the room and went to the nursing station. Ruth spoke in hushed tones. "We were visiting Margaret Woodson. Can you give us an update on her condition?"

The nurses explained that Margaret had completed her physical therapy appointment for the day and was making great progress. She was tired and still in some pain. The nurse said it was expected after surgery and with the rehab schedule. Gone were the days of lying in bed waiting for a broken hip to heal. Patients were up and moving within 1-2 days. Margaret's surgery had been four days ago. The nurse explained that she could go home from the rehab facility as soon as they could confirm that someone would be available to help care for her at home. *Guess that's me,* Dani thought.

"You're sure she's going to be okay?" Danielle asked. The nurse's confirmation made Danielle let out a breath. Her aunt wouldn't die. It would be 11-12 weeks before she could resume full activities, like working at the bakery, but she would recover. Dani was surprised how relieved she was to hear the positive prognosis. She barely knew her aunt, but she wasn't ready to lose her, either. Already grateful for the opportunity to see her and the warm reception, she gave quick thanks to God. *If Ruth hadn't called, I might never have seen Aunt Maggie again.*

Chapter 5

After visiting Margaret, Ruth dropped Danielle back off at her aunt's house. Danielle found a guest room and unpacked into the small dresser. While folding her beloved screen tees, she remembered her commitment to not highlight her geekiness. She set them at the bottom of the stack. Then, she collapsed into the bed, and Loki jumped up on top of her and settled in. Getting up at three to make her five-thirty flight had her feeling her stamina bar was flashing empty like the video game characters she played.

In the morning, she felt like an intruder in the cozy house. It so clearly belonged to someone else. There were touches of Margaret everywhere, and Danielle tried to learn what she could from the pictures and knickknacks in the space. On the mantle rested frames with photos from years ago. Dani recognized her mother as a young girl, dancing with Margaret, huge grins filling their faces. A few others with a couple that could only be Dani's grandparents. She wondered what they were like. She never got to meet them. Whatever drove her mother away from home had been enough that she never came back. Or maybe she wasn't welcome.

Not wanting to linger on the negative thought, Danielle moved on. She examined book titles and laughed at the collection of VHS tapes - romantic comedies from the 90s. Danielle hadn't watched a movie on VHS since she was a girl. There was a basket next to a recliner with three skeins of yarn and a partially-finished baby blanket. The crochet hook was still slipped through the last loop. Knowing her aunt shared the same hobby released the tension from her shoulders. They could connect over something, at least.

She spotted car keys on a hook in the kitchen and looked in the garage, pleased to see a little blue Honda civic. No public transportation in Minden, that was sure. At least she wouldn't be trapped. She grabbed the keys and a bottle of water from the fridge and decided to explore.

Ten minutes later, she'd seen everything Minden offered. She drove down Main Street, spotting the bakery sitting next door to a busy little restaurant

the sign proclaimed as B&Js Bistro. There was a bar
and grill called Bulldog's down the block. A church
and a park at the end of the road before the
'downtown' district gave way to cute, well-kept
residential houses, much like the one Margaret
owned a few blocks south of Main Street. She
turned around in someone's driveway and headed
back toward the bakery. Dani removed the keys
from the ignition and walked up. She'd been
dreaming about the bakery since she got the call
from Ruth. Yes, she wanted to come help Aunt
Maggie. And yes, having a real family again was
appealing. But she was broke and she missed
working at the bakery with Casey. If she was being
honest with herself - the chance to run the bakery
for Margaret was the reason she came to Minden.

She looked at the display in the window,
admiring her aunt's delicately decorated sugar
cookies in summer designs: beach balls, flip-flops,
and glasses of icy lemonade. She cupped her hands
against the glass and tried to look beyond the
display case. There were four small tables and a
larger bakery case off to the side. Behind the case,
Danielle couldn't see the workspace.

Crossing her fingers, she placed a key in the
lock. *Please be the one I need.* She exhaled and
smiled broadly when the key rotated and the door
gave way when she pulled on the handle. The space
smelled familiar. Yeast and sugar, chocolate and

vanilla. There was still dough covered by a cloth towel and left to rise. There was a step stool placed in front of a bank of cabinets, the uppermost cabinet door still open and a box of cookie cutters open and spilling across the floor. *Margaret must have fallen off the step stool. Ouch.*

Danielle picked up the cookie cutters and set them back in the box. She wandered the space, running her hand across the work tables. A small mess remained from the abrupt departure of Margaret. When she spotted the industrial sized Hobart mixer, she nearly danced. Even when Cupcakes by Casey opened at the storefront location, Casey didn't have the money for the industrial mixer, and they worked with residential stand mixers running around the clock.

She tasted the frosting from the fridge, pleased at the buttery sweetness. *I guess Aunt Maggie knows what she's doing.* Danielle found herself full of questions for her mother's mother. How long had she owned the bakery? Did she have it when she came to visit all those years ago? Why hadn't she come again? Why hadn't her mom wanted them to visit Indiana? Now that her mom was gone, she might never know the whole story. But maybe her aunt had answers. Eventually, she'd get them. For now, she needed to clean and hang a sign on the door. She found supplies in the small office made a sign after studying the posted hours. Today was

Thursday, so she wrote the note announcing the bakery would reopen Monday for limited hours. That should be enough time to get her aunt moved home and settled in.

After she tidied and washed dishes and tossed baked goods that would dry out by Monday, she grabbed the keys and made her way to the door. Her hand on the cool, metal handle, she paused and looked back at the bakery. It was lit only by the sunlight coming through the front windows. She listened, and in the silence her heart seemed to take a breath. It felt good here. One corner of her mouth lifted and she pushed the door open, stepping into the engulfing humidity and heat.

Despite the tasting she had done while cleaning and familiarizing herself with the bakery, she needed real food. She walked the few steps and decided B&J Bistro must be the place to be. Several tables were visible through the window, along with a small seating area with couches and chairs. A man on a laptop occupied one small table, and four high-school-aged girls drank iced coffees and chatted at the couch. *This doesn't look too bad. I wonder if they have vegetarian options.* Danielle ate fish occasionally, but preferred to stick with non-meat entrees. It was a side bonus that meat was usually the most expensive part of any meal, and she could save money by avoiding it most of the time.

Dani walked in to the bistro and bells jingled,

announcing her arrival. Every head in the diner turned, and she could almost hear the screech of a vinyl record being cut off. Frozen, Dani could feel the good mood and confidence that had followed her from the bakery slink back out the door behind her. A voice in her head was yelling "Retreat, retreat!" when she heard a cheery voice from the back of the room.

"Good morning! Come on in and have a seat. I'll be right over." Gradually, the buzz of conversation returned and Dani took a breath before finding an empty table.

She whispered to herself, "You roll for stealth." Shaking her head, she studied the chalkboard menu behind the counter.

"You roll a natural one."

Her eyes widened and she turned to see a man with dark hair and dark eyes framed in thick black glasses looking at her and grinning.

"I'm sorry, what?" She realized this super cute guy heard her talk to herself and refer to a role-playing game she'd dabbled in for years. Hadn't she promised to keep her weird hobbies under wraps in this new city?

"I said, you roll a one. That entrance? Anything but stealthy. But I'm hoping if I do a charisma check, I might persuade you to join me for lunch."

What is happening right now? He'd heard her and he'd responded in the secret language only gamers understood. He looked harmless enough. His dirty shirt and muddy boots didn't scream 'gamer', but was that a Zelda Triforce?

"Ummm," she stalled. *What am I supposed to say?*

He extended his hand toward her. "I'm Mark."

Before she thought about it, her hand was in his and she responded, "Dani."

"Nice to meet you, Dani." After convincing her to join him at the next table, Mark sat across from her with a smile on his face. It was unnerving. *Why was he looking at her like that?*

"Chrissy--she owns this place--has started getting a lot of interstate traffic. Tell me you're not just passing through?"

"Actually, no. I'm here to help my aunt. She fell and broke her hip. I guess I'll be here for three months or so."

"Oh, do you mean Margaret?"

"Yeah! Do you know her?"

"Sure. This is Minden, after all. Besides, she makes the best red velvet cake I've ever had. My mom gets me one every year for my birthday."

"That's really sweet."

"Hey, Mark. Who's your friend?" The waitress came to the table, brown hair dyed with pink at the ends fell to her shoulders.

Mark introduced Dani to Holly, and they placed their orders. The young waitress was welcoming and Danielle started to relax.

"So, you play Quest?"

Dani tried to explain, "Well, I don't play it much anymore. But once upon a time? Yeah, I did." She ducked her head, embarrassed to admit her hobbies even to a fellow gamer.

"That's awesome." When she looked up, Mark was giving her another wide smile. He talked with his hands as he continued. "I mean, I haven't played lately, either. But it's almost impossible to find people around here who don't look at you like a heathen when you say something about elves or wizards!"

"It's that way everywhere. Totally normal conversation until someone mentions how much the JELL-O salad resembles Jigglypuff!" She gave an exaggerated look of bewilderment.

Mark laughed, his rich tenor filling the space surrounding their small table. She looked around, as though she might see the sound in the air like an action word in a comic book.

By the time Holly came to take her order, Danielle and Mark were deep in conversation about the latest superhero movie. They debated the accuracy of the movie compared to the comic-book characters. Mark was a purist, but Danielle was okay with the creative license taken by the filmmakers. It made the story appeal to a broader audience.

"You are telling me you have a cat named Loki?" Mark raised an eyebrow.

Danielle nodded. "That's exactly what I'm telling you."

"Is he evil and determined to destroy the world to spite his brother?"

"Absolutely. Total god of mischief. But he likes to snuggle, so I let him get away with it." Danielle gave a crooked smile.

Mark's quiet laughter rang in the air, and Danielle felt a thrill from her smiling cheeks down to the balls of her feet. She could not help but chuckle, too. When she was particularly proud of a joke she made, Danielle was always the first to laugh. She wished she could be the person who delivered a monotone line and had a deadpan expression while the people around her cracked up, but she laughed even harder than anyone listening. But Mark had laughed. Perhaps she wasn't the only one who found herself entertaining.

Holly delivered their food. A barbecue sandwich for Mark and a Mediterranean salad for Danielle. It looked delicious. She had debated ordering it, unsure of the quality of food in this small restaurant in the middle of Minden. Mark reassured her the food was top notch and the produce fresh from local farms. He pointed to the note at the bottom of the menu which said "All fruits, vegetables, and herbs are proudly provided by Bloom's Farm, located 20 miles north of Minden." Along with "When available, all meat and dairy are sourced from organic, local suppliers." And the one that made her nervous: "All breads and desserts are the amazing creations of The Rolling Pin bakery, located next door."

She hadn't expected to find a place so progressive in this minuscule dot on the map. Danielle watched Mark bow his head and close his eyes before digging into his sandwich. Was he praying? Oh man, she was a goner. This guy was cute, funny, knew comic books and Japanese cartoons, and he just casually, and without fanfare, took a moment to thank God for his food next to a complete stranger. It had never even crossed her mind, she realized ashamed. She put down her water and spoke her own thank you to her heavenly father. She added a quick note of thanks for her new friend, Mark. When she looked up, Mark was watching her and smiling behind the large sandwich he held in his hand. She smiled back and picked up her fork. She stabbed an olive and popped it into her mouth.

The olive slipped to the back of her throat and her eyes widened. She couldn't breathe. A violent cough brought the olive to the front of her mouth again. She coughed repeatedly, trying to catch her breath and clear the terrifying sensation of something stuck in her windpipe. She spit the olive into her napkin and continued to cough as her tears streamed from the outside corners of her eyes. Mark was out of his chair and standing next to hers.

"I'm okay, I'm okay." Another cough. She cleared her throat roughly. Mark reached over and grabbed her water, offering it by holding it in front of her. She grabbed it, grateful for the gesture. After a quick drink, she coughed a few more times and wiped her eyes. Oh my gosh, this is so humiliating. You would think I hadn't been eating solid food for 30 years.

"Are you sure you are okay?" Mark's voice was quiet and his hand rested on her upper back. He rubbed small circles just below the collar of her shirt. She nodded, but the unshakable sensation that something was still in her throat remained. She swallowed painfully, trying to remove it. He must think I'm a total klutz. Never mind that it was true. Didn't make it any less embarrassing. He has no idea what a train wreck my life is. Maybe this was a sign that she shouldn't get her hopes up. Mark said he was a teacher. He had a family and a good job. He had an entire community of people who loved him, if all the waves and smiles he had received from patrons of the restaurant were any indication. She, on the other hand, was here only by chance. No money, no job, no family. Unless you counted Aunt Maggie, which to be honest, she didn't. She and Mark could be friends while she was in Minden. But anything more was just asking for trouble.

Mark removed his hand, the comforting warmth of the gesture replaced with cool air. She had to make sure she did not fall for him.

"Well, now that my near demise is over," she let out a nervous laugh, "you mentioned you had brothers? Tell me about them?"

Mark sighed and rolled his eyes. "There are five of us. Daniel is the oldest. He plays defensive linebacker for the Boston Revolutionaries."

"Is that baseball?" Danielle took a stab. Sports were not her thing.

Mark responded, "Football," he corrected, "but it doesn't matter. It should tell you most of what you need to know. He's always been a jock. One track mind. Or maybe two: sports, girls." He held up two fingers in emphasis. "Then there's Malachi. He's like Tony Stark. Crazy smart, CEO of a tech company out in San Francisco."

"Really? That's where I'm from. What company?"

"Dawson Dynamics."

"Oh, wow. My friend Liz, from Knit Night works
there."

"Small world. I wonder if she knows him?" At Dani's shrug, he continued. "Anyway, next is Stephen. I think of him as Captain America. He's a pastor over in Terre Haute, about 45 minutes away.

He and I are pretty close. It helps that we both stayed around this area, but we always had more in common. He is really creative, plays guitar and all that. Then comes me, and the youngest is Gideon. He just graduated from IU with his degree in journalism. I think he envisions being the next hard-hitting investigative journalist. But he's also the baby and hasn't had to work hard for much. He's still interviewing for jobs, but seems to think he's too good for the ones offered." Mark shook his head and Danielle nodded.

"I know people like that back home. As though the manager position will be handed to them with no experience. Or that they can earn a living by working twenty hours a week and taking weekend trips to wine country all the time."

"Right? I keep trying to teach my kids that hard work will get farther in life than anything else. What is that quote? I find that the harder I work, the luckier I am."

"Whoa, I like that. I've never heard that."

"Those are my brothers, though. We haven't all been together in a long time. Between Malachi on the West Coast and Daniel on the East, it's difficult. When we are together, or even missing one or two, it's loud and crazy. My mom loves it."

"Oh my gosh, I never even considered your poor mother. I can't imagine what it would be like to raise five boys!"

"Yeah, she is pretty amazing. I remember when we were teenagers, she bought milk three gallons at a time and went through the grocery store with two shopping carts. Especially during football season. My mom lived in the kitchen."

"Is she still nearby?"

"Yeah, she and my dad still live in Minden. About a seven-minute walk from here."

Danielle experienced a stab of envy. Her mom had been her best friend. Since she was gone, Danielle felt her absence like a physical pit. Her mom would have been the one she called after getting let go from the bakery. She would've been the one Danielle called after her flight to Indiana, to complain about airport security and the cost of an airline ticket. Instead, Danielle didn't have that person anymore. She had friends. But she didn't want to call her friends 'just to chat' every single day. That's what she *had done* until her mom died. She would give anything to be a seven-minute walk away. She hoped Mark knew how lucky he was.

"What's wrong?" Mark's head tilted left; his eyes on her. She forced a smile and shook her head. "Nothing. Just thinking." She shrugged off the melancholy and asked another question to get Mark talking again.

Chapter 6

After lunch at the bistro, Danielle drove back to
the rehab facility. Again, she found her aunt asleep
in the room. Danielle sat on the armchair and began
to play with the yarn and crochet hooks she'd
brought for Margaret. She had debated bringing
them, unsure if Aunt Maggie would be interested or
have the energy to work on anything. In the end,
Danielle figured she would want to crochet if she
were in a strange place. She heard the blankets
rustle, and a sharp gasp followed by a low moan.
Putting down the crochet, she approached the bed
where Margaret lay, eyes open. "Hey Aunt
Maggie."

"Danielle. You're still here?"

"Yes, I am. I'm not going anywhere." Trying not

to overwhelm her aunt with information, she didn't give any update on the bakery or plans to come home. "How are you feeling? Do you need anything?"

"Could you get a nurse for me?" Danielle nodded and went out to find a nurse. After letting them know her aunt was awake, she returned to find her sitting on the edge of the bed. She was looking at the small sphere Danielle had crocheted while waiting. "I may forget a few things, but I'm pretty sure I didn't make this. Which means you must have."

Danielle resisted the urge to lower her chin. Instead, she stated with pride, "My mom taught me to crochet."

Margaret fingered the soft yarn and nodded slowly. "Our mother taught both of us. I didn't know Bea kept crocheting after she left home."

"She did. Sometimes I think it made her sad, but she could never seem to give it up entirely." Danielle thought back to her mom in front of the TV. She remembered watching her mom just study the project she was working on, running her fingers over it. Was she thinking of her mom and remembering home with every row? "Why did she leave, Aunt Maggie?" She looked at Margaret for an answer. She shook her head and opened her mouth, but a woman with brassy blonde hair entered the room and drew her attention.

"Did you have a great nap, Margaret? I'm sure you needed one after that workout from Dr. Grant." The nurse looked at Danielle and continued, "Margaret is doing awesome at her physical therapy appointments. "Are you a friend?"

Margaret spoke up, "This is my niece, Danielle."

Her own heart swelled once again at the realization that she was someone's something. But Danielle noticed the double-take of the nurse. The woman was looking between herself and her aunt, looking for the family resemblance.

"Well, that's just wonderful." It took her a long time to find those three words. Danielle was not surprised. People often assumed adoption when she was out with her mother. Despite many shared features, they couldn't see past the color of her skin to the similar eyes of her mother.

The nurse help Margaret off the bed and positioned her walker. Danielle watched as her aunt shuffled to the bathroom located near the entry of the room. Despite having broken her hip days before, Margaret was walking on her own. Danielle was tempted to question whether walking was something her grandmother should be doing already, but figured the doctors and nurses knew what they were doing. She certainly had no idea what was proper. Not something they covered in her six months of culinary school. When Margaret came

58

out the restroom, the nurse help ease her into the armchair and Danielle sat on the edge of the bed. The nurse gave her a small cup with several pills in it and a glass of water.

"You will take one more dose later tonight, and the night shift should bring you some around 2 AM. Okay Margaret?"

"Okay, dear."

"How's your pain level, is it okay?" Margaret swallowed the pill with a grimace. "I'm fine, Sharon. Thank you." She waved a hand toward the hallway.

"Okay, okay. Dinner in two hours."

"You know I don't want any of their fake-sugar dessert. And none of that fake butter, either."

Danielle covered her smile with a casual chin scratch as Sharon left. Apparently, Maggie was feisty. Danielle couldn't blame her; real sugar and butter were the cornerstones of any bakery. Aunt Maggie turned and spoke to Danielle. "I can't wait to get back to my kitchen and whip up real bread. The dinner rolls here taste like cardboard."

Danielle laughed. "Well, how about we figure out what we need to bust you outta here." Danielle tried to remember what Ruth had said. It should be soon. "I can get things ready at your house. Whenever you get the okay from the doctors, you can come home."

"Dani, dear. I'm sure glad you're here, but don't

you have somewhere to be? A family? A Job? I can't possibly ask you to put your life on hold to take care of an old woman like me."

"Actually, I don't. I'm pretty sure God designed it this way, though. Being here and helping you is exactly what I'm supposed to be doing. I bet you didn't even know that I was working at a bakery in California until last week?"

"Well, isn't that wonderful? Do you think you can handle my open orders? I have two cakes scheduled, and I'm sure Chrissy is running low on everything at the bistro. Oh my, I never even called her." Her aunt started to breathe quickly and Danielle saw her starting to get worked up.

"Shhh, it's okay. Miss Ruth said that Chrissy and Norm had it handled through backup suppliers. The bistro is fine. I saw on your calendar that you don't have any cakes until next week. I already posted a sign at the bakery saying that it would be open next week."

At the news, Margaret melted into the recliner. "Good, good." She closed her eyes and her breathing slowed to an easy, even pace. Danielle watched her face relax and knew her aunt had fallen asleep. That was enough for one day, anyway. She leaned over the chair and kissed her forehead. To her hairline, Danielle whispered, "See you tomorrow."

*****

Mark sat atop the expensive zero-turn-radius lawn mower, maneuvering around the short trees and zipping along the fence line. The ninety-degree heat was unforgiving, even though it was before noon. He'd forgotten the level of hard work Luke's landscaping business required. He hadn't been this hot and sweaty since last summer, but mowing was the easy part. Trimming and weed-eating were time consuming, but they made all the difference. Luke told him to add his parents' house to the route first thing this morning, and Mark had done theirs and two other properties so far.

Luke's business handled both lawn and garden maintenance as well as landscaping and hardscaping. Mark hated building retaining walls and hauling bags of river rock from trailer to flower bed. It was a rigorous workout, and oh, did he pay the next day! *If only teaching paid better,* he mused.

Mowing gave him plenty of time to think about Danielle and their chance meeting at the bistro. When the last pass on the yard was complete, he guided the lawn mower back into the trailer. After killing the engine, he removed his earmuffs just in time to hear the chime of his cell phone interrupting the sudden silence. Without looking, he answered, "This is Mark."

"Hi, Mr. Dawson. This is Mr. Morton." *Well,*

61

that's odd. Why would his friend and boss be so formal?

"Hi, Steve. How are you?"

"I'm okay. Been better actually."

Mental alarm bells were ringing. "What's going on?" It was unusual for him to get a call from the school in the summer, especially from the principal instead of an administrator.

He heard his friend take a deep breath. "Well, I need you to come in. I've got something serious to discuss with you."

"Ummm, okay. Can you give me any more information?" Maybe Steve could shed light on the situation. They'd worked together for six years and bonded as the only two male teachers at the middle school.

Steve clicked his tongue. "I'm sorry, it will have to wait until we speak in person."

Mark frowned. This didn't sound good. In fact, this sounded very, very bad. "Okay, when do you want to meet?"

"As soon as possible. This isn't something I want to prolong." What could be so important that a spur-of-the-moment visit was necessary? This had to be serious. Steve was as cool and collected as anyone Mark had ever met. He was a welcome pillar of steadfast composure in the sometimes-chaotic world of education. But Mark could tell something had him rattled.

"Sure thing. Let me check with Luke, but I think I can come in later today."

He heard Mr. Morton's exhale of relief. "Great. I'll see you soon."

He hung up and immediately called Luke, explaining the mysterious call. When he had the green light, he finished trimming the property he was working on and drove the truck back to Luke's supply yard.

Swinging by his house to grab lunch, a quick shower, and to change into his school clothes, Mark made it to the school an hour and a half after hanging up with Mr. Morton. An uneasy feeling followed him every step of the way, so close he could feel it stepping on his heels. He flipped through his end of the school-year checklist. Had he forgotten to submit grades? Or left his Continuing Education credits unfiled? By the time he entered the administration office at the middle school, he was sweating nervously and convinced he was going to be let go. Budget cuts or something equally offensive.

The secretary barely made eye contact with him as she waved him back to Mr. Morton's office. Mark remembered more conversations in this office than he could count. Books filled a wall of shelves, and even more were stacked on a chair in the corner. There were volumes on education, leadership, and Steve's guilty pleasure: old Louis

L'Amour westerns. Steve's eyes darted around the room, resting for a moment through the glass to the secretary outside before finally landing on Mark. Mark noticed bloodshot eyes surrounded by dark circles. Steve's clothes were rumpled and his hair was unkempt.

"Jeez, man. You look like you haven't slept in days." Mark watched his friend and mentor give a pained smile. "Just spill it." Mark hated the anxious look he saw etched on Steve's face.

Steve rubbed his face with both hands and sighed heavily before gesturing to a chair. "Take a seat."

Mark settled in and crossed an ankle over his knee, his slim-fit dark jeans slipping up to reveal Superman socks above his gray suede oxfords. He raised an eyebrow at Steve.

"Okay. I'm just going to come out and say it." Steve sat up straight in his chair and took a heavy breath. "Here's the deal. There is a student and parent accusing you of inappropriate contact." Steve was using the tone he used at a staff meeting. All business.

Mark felt himself flinch and his mouth opened and closed, no words escaping. "What?" He straightened in the chair and his throat tightened. He spoke into the haze clouding his vision and thoughts. "Who would say that?"

"I'm sorry. I can't actually tell you anything

else," Steve explained in apologetic but firm tones.

This can't be happening. "I don't - this doesn't make any sense, Steve. I'm a good teacher. Shoot, I'm a great teacher. Whatever they are saying, it's a lie." He felt the heat rising through his chest and neck and his pulse raced. The immediate shock was replaced with a staunch disbelief and outrage at the accusation. He stood and began pacing the small room. One, two, three steps. Turn. One, two, three steps.

"I know you are, Mark. But I have no choice. I have to investigate. We are lucky they waited until summer break to make the allegation, because otherwise I would have had to suspend you from the classroom until the investigation concluded."

He whirled toward Steve's chair behind the desk. "Are you kidding me? That's all it takes for a good teacher to be kicked out of his own classroom?"

Steve held up a hand against the verbal assault. "I know it seems insulting," Mark scoffed at the inadequate term, "but we have to take these things seriously. There are too many stories of students being taken advantage of." Mark began to protest and Steve talked over him. "I'm not saying you did anything. But I don't have a choice. Look, for now, nothing changes. Just continue to work your summer job. Contact your union rep and see what they need from you. We will investigate and hopefully the accusations are resolved quickly and quietly."

Mark rubbed a hand down his face and tried to press away the burning sensation behind his eyes. "Dang it, Steve. I deserve to know who is saying this. Why would they fabricate this?"

Steve's features softened and he spoke gently. "I really wish I could, Mark. It's going to be okay. We'll get to the bottom of this."

Mark barely remembered walking out of the office. Once he reached his car, he sat in the stifling warmth, shutting the door but not turning on the car. Then, he broke down. Mark couldn't remember the last time he cried. Maybe when his Nonna died. But now? His entire career was in jeopardy and he didn't even know why.

According to Mr. Morton, there was nothing he could do except wait. Tears rolled down his cheeks unchecked and he inhaled and released several shaky breaths. He cried out to God; wordless, desperate pleas for providence and truth to prevail. *I'm a teacher, God. What am I without that? It's been my dream forever. Who is trying to destroy my reputation?*

It sounded so trite to remind himself to trust God. It seemed like the ground had fallen out from under him in the last twenty minutes, leaving him suspended above a chasm threatening to swallow him whole. *I didn't do this. I haven't done anything.*

Could he trust that the investigation would show the truth? What if this became public? Early in his career, he'd been warned even false allegations would follow someone forever. Even proven innocent, he knew of male teachers who had to move states away to get a job. He'd aspired to be a teacher since he was an awkward preteen looking for a role model. The thought of never teaching again was heart breaking! He wracked his brain for ideas as to which student would accuse him of something so horrendous. What did 'inappropriate contact' even mean? Possibilities flashed through his mind, each one worse than the next. What if? What now? Who? When? Why?

Several minutes later he started the car, no closer to the answers that could bring peace to his troubled thoughts.

Chapter 7

All weekend, Danielle followed Margaret's recipes and prepared orders for the bistro. Ruth's boyfriend, Norm, prioritized which types of breads and desserts they needed. For Danielle, talking with the mirific chef was almost like being back in culinary school. Norm had been an executive chef in Chicago for his entire career before moving back to the area. Initially, he planned to use the backup supplier until Margaret could return to work, but she convinced him she could handle it. She hoped it was true.

She made dozens of practice loaves of the 5-grain whole wheat to get the right chewy consistency and the right balance of salt and sweetness. Cupcakes by Casey had a small focus, and Danielle was out of practice on breads and cookies. Margaret's sourdough starter was in the fridge and Danielle grilled her aunt with questions, running back and forth from the bakery to the house a few blocks away. In theory, she knew how to handle sourdough, but in practice it freaked her out a little. 'Feeding' the starter and making sure she had the right amount each day seemed more like biology class than baking. She was grateful that her aunt had moved back to Minden and out of the rehab facility. Judging by how she raved about Danielle's cooking, Aunt Maggie was glad, too.

Visitors came in droves after Margaret settled at home. Danielle's head was spinning from all the names and faces. Apparently all 500 people in Minden knew each other extremely well, not to mention the surrounding communities and farms. She escaped to the bakery, choosing to spend her time with the familiar instruments rather than as a constant source of questions. More than once, when Maggie had introduced her as Beatrice's daughter, the older visitor had given her a look of disbelief. The look was usually followed by a shake of their head or a vague comment like, "I always wondered what happened to Bea."

Much to Danielle's dismay, her aunt still hadn't talked about it. Every time they were in conversation and Danielle felt like she was close to getting something from her, Margaret just pressed her lips together and changed the subject or said "I'm too tired right now, sweetie."

Plus, she hadn't seen or heard from Mark since they met at the bistro. Danielle was taking out her frustration by kneading a poor batch of dough that had done nothing to deserve her rough handling. Had he changed his mind? It would make sense. Maybe his second thoughts got the best of him and he realized that she was nowhere near his league. It wouldn't be the first time. Despite her good grades, Christian upbringing, and general well-behaved nature; the parents of her high school boyfriend forbade him from seeing her. She never got much of an explanation, but James had acted apologetic about it, but hadn't pressed the issue. She figured he agreed. For some unexplained reason, she wasn't good enough for their precious baby.

But she was totally over it. Never even crossed her mind. Except in nearly every episode of self-doubt and poor self-esteem she'd ever had since. It still ate at her; the judgment of someone she barely knew who had seen her and decided immediately her worth was less than desirable. Despite the hundreds of small reminders God had given her since that time in high school that her worth was far above rubies; it still hurt.

She looked down and tested the dough with her finger. Over-kneaded. "Where is your head at, Dani?" She posed the question to the empty kitchen.

"Looks like it is still safely attached to your neck and shoulders, I'd say."

The voice made her jump and she turned with a hand over her racing heart to find Mark standing at the counter behind her. "Don't sneak up on a person like that! Are you crazy?"

Mark shrugged. "Depends who you ask, probably." She shook her head at his comment and picked up the dough and threw it in a nearby trashcan. He raised an eyebrow. "Aren't you supposed to bake that?"

She pulled a spoon out of the flour bin and started carefully spooning flour into a bowl on a small scale. "I ruined that batch. Not worth baking it only for it to be rock-hard and dry."

"Whoa. You can tell how the bread would turn out before you even finish it?"

"Lots of practice. I got distracted and kneaded it too long. The mixer works better, but I like to do it by hand. Plus, Aunt Maggie insists." She finished adding the ingredients in the small bowl, then added them to the mixer. She sprinkled some flour on the stainless steel work table and studied the dough as it turned around the dough hook for a minute, deciding to only finish it by hand this time. *That's good enough, right?*

She felt Mark watching her as she removed the dough from the mixer, still slightly tacky. The dough would come together in her hands. To fill the silence, she started narrating her actions. "I'm just going to press and release and roll this around for about ten minutes until it is nice and elastic."

As she played with the dough, her eyes met Mark's across the counter.

"Did Margaret teach you all this?"

"No. Actually, until I got out here, I hadn't seen Aunt Maggie since I was six or seven years old. My mom wasn't exactly close with her Indiana roots."

"So, where did you learn?"

"I went to culinary school for about six months, but otherwise it was mostly self-taught. Here," she gestured to the space next to her, "wash your hands and come feel this." The dough was almost done. She wanted Mark to experience the moments when the dough went from 'not ready' to 'perfect'.

He followed directions and stood next to her. Her body was hyper aware of his proximity, but she forced herself to focus on the task at hand.

"Take this." She took a step to the side and let him take her position directly in front of the dough. "Lift the back half, here." She guided his hands and continued, "then press it into the front half." Her fingers grazed the back of his hands and arms as she showed him how to work the dough. "Do you feel how it bounces back after you push in? Keep going." She gently corrected him, "Press with the heel of your hand, not your fingers. There you go."

He gave her a hesitant smile. "Am I doing it

right?"

"You're doing great," she said honestly. "Let me feel it." The dough bounced back when she poked with a finger. "Okay, great. Now we form it into a smooth ball." She took control again and shaped the dough into a ball. Then, she placed it into a large bowl and covered it with a thin towel. "There. About an hour and it will be ready for the next step."

"Baking it?"

"Not quite. We've got to knock it down and knead it again. Then it will rise again before baking."

"Wow. That's a lot of work."

She nodded. "But it'll be worth it. It's pretty hard to beat fresh homemade bread slathered with butter."

Mark let his tongue fall out on side of his mouth in an exaggerated drooling gesture. "Mind if I stick around to try it?"

Danielle's eyes widened. He wanted to stay around the bakery for the next two hours? Her to-do list flicked through her mind. Tomorrow she would officially be open for business. She still needed to make cookies, dinner rolls, and a couple of batches of cupcakes so the display case wouldn't be completely empty. She'd skipped church this morning and was off to a good start on the breads.

"You can stay, but I'm going to put you to

work."

He held up his flour-dusted hands. "My hands are yours."

*****

Helping Danielle at the bakery was exactly the distraction he needed. After the bombshell Steve had dropped on him Friday, he'd wasted his Saturday battling his way through a video game he'd already beaten once. It was a distraction, but not a good one. It was too easy to press pause and let himself get lost in the downward spiral of self-pity. He felt like David in the Psalms, his enemies closing around him with no relief.

The worst part was it could take weeks or months to clear his name. Until then, he was in limbo. He knew he probably shouldn't be here, getting cozy with Dani when the rest of his life might fall apart at any moment. But he couldn't help it. The decision to go into the closed bakery had been pure impulse when his wandering stroll after church led him down Main Street and he spotted the familiar sign for "The Rolling Pin". The bakery had the same sign since he was a little boy. He remembered leaving sticky fingerprints on the door after Margaret gave his mother seven cupcakes for the price of four, like she always did.

He and his brothers would sit at the miniscule

tables inside and enjoy their cupcakes while his mom would talk with Margaret. More accurately, they ate their frosting and mostly left the cake untouched. Back then, he thought she was graciously letting them eat their cupcakes before leaving, but now he realized she was probably grateful for the distraction and the adult conversation. When Daniel and Mark were old enough, she let the boys walk to the park and run off the sugar they had devoured.

Main Street in Minden hadn't changed a lot during the years since he was a kid. If anything, the area was revitalized. The craft store opened a few years ago in the abandoned building which housed a small grocery store in the seventies. The community had received a grant to open a small library, which now resided in a converted residential house at the edge of the business district. He remembered riding bikes from his house to the QuikStop nearly every day with change in his pocket to buy candy and soda. Later, it was bumming rides from Daniel in his car, and then giving those same rides to his younger siblings.

Minden was a great place to raise a family. He hadn't considered living anywhere else. But if this mess at school became public, what would happen? Even false allegations could ruin his career. He'd forever be associated with a scandal in the small town of Minden. People here had a long memory.

Half the residents had witnessed Malachi and him streaking through downtown at fourteen after losing a bet with Daniel. He'd never live that down; he still turned bright red when someone brought it up. Accusations of abusing a student would hover in the air around him like a swarm of gnats, filling every room with whispers and curious glances. People here would always wonder if it had actually been true, despite the findings. He'd always taken a future here for granted. Until now, when malicious rumors threatened to steal it from him.

He watched Danielle move around the kitchen. She moved with purpose, pulling ingredients from the shelves and checking recipes on dirty, handwritten notecards. It wasn't fair that the day after he met someone he'd been waiting his entire life for, he was blindsided with the accusations. Could he ignore the pending investigation and simply get to know Danielle? She had no reason to believe in his innocence. He couldn't tell her about the situation. He hadn't even told his parents or his brothers yet. Even Todd, who he considered his best friend, was still in the dark. That had to change. But he didn't want to admit to anyone that he was under investigation, even though it was completely fabricated.

Instead, he would busy himself helping Danielle and hoping he could get close enough to have her hands on his again, like they were while he kneaded the dough. She'd been so close, their hips nearly touching. Now, she was across the room, humming softly to the radio. Occasionally, actual words emerged from her lips. The radio wasn't loud, just background music he barely heard when she turned on the mixers.

He rubbed his hand together and the cloud of flour reminded him he should be helping. "What can I do?"

Danielle looked up from the recipe card, blinking back to focus, as though she had forgotten he was there. *Well, that was flattering.* How long had his thoughts wandered?

She glanced around the kitchen. "Why don't you make the buttercream?"

"Ummm, sure. Just tell me how."

"Super easy. Take one of those blocks of butter and throw it in the small mixer. Then add powdered sugar. About 10 cups. One cup at a time. And about three tablespoons of vanilla." She handed him a bottle of clear liquid. *Isn't vanilla brown?* The label revealed the clear liquid was vanilla, so he looked for the butter where Danielle had gestured. Expecting to see sticks, he was surprised to find butter wrapped in something akin to the size of a brick. *Oh man, my brothers would have gone crazy for this much frosting back in the day.*

For the next four hours, Mark helped as much as he could. Mostly, he ended up relegated to dish duty, washing mixing bowls and the little metal cones Danielle used to apply frosting to cupcakes in intricate patterns. He made a huge batch of frosting and was astonished when he had to make a second batch the same size.

"Tomorrow is the big day, huh?" Danielle was arranging cookies on a tray, and he was wiping down the counters.

She stepped back, studying her handiwork. She took a deep breath, and he watched her placed her hands at the small of her back and lean into them. It was no surprise that she was tired and sore. She'd been working since the early morning, and he hadn't even seen her take a break.

"Tomorrow is the big day," she confirmed. The desire to be close enough that he could reach over and rub the tension from her shoulders hit him. Worry etched deep lines in her forehead as she examined the display case and rearranged the cookies for the third time.

"It's going to be great. Everyone in Minden has missed having The Rolling Pin open. Plus, you are every bit as good as Margaret. Maybe even better. And if you tell her I said that, I'll deny it to my dying breath."

He warmed when she laughed, pleased at his successful effort to relax her.

"Thanks, Mark. I appreciate your help today. I would have been here all night if you hadn't stopped by. Everything for the Bistro is done and at least enough to make the display case not seem completely barren when people come in tomorrow."

"Try not to worry. Why don't we get out of here and grab some dinner to take your mind off things?" More time with her would keep his mind occupied, too.

"Okay. I need to drop these off and stop by to see Aunt Maggie, but then I should be free."

He supposed it was unreasonable for the delay to disappoint him, but it did. He should probably change clothes, anyway. The slim khakis and checkered button down he'd worn to church were specked with butter and sugar and evidence of the incident he'd had with the food coloring gel. He'd been too stubborn to accept the apron Danielle had offered with a shy smile about an hour into his baking adventure. Next time, he'd wear the apron and protect his clothes.

"Sounds good. I'll run home and change so no one thinks I've been stabbed," he gestured at the bright red food coloring stain across his abdomen, "and pick you up at Margaret's around seven."

They took the large cart of croissants, breads, cookies and brownies outside and rolled it to the back door of B&J Bistro. Norm let them in and greeted them both warmly as he welcomed them into the air conditioning. After thirty seconds in the stifling heat of the summer, even the usually oven-warmed air of the restaurant kitchen felt cool.

"Ah! Excellent. I've got a summer chicken salad special in mind for tomorrow, and these croissants will be the perfect base!" Danielle smiled and Mark watched her with admiration as she interacted with the experienced chef. She knew her stuff. She spoke softly, deferring to Norm's larger personality, but she talked him through the baked goods with obvious pride.

"I made a five-grain honey wheat based on Maggie's recipe, but I also included one loaf of this sunflower, oat, and flaxseed bread. It's my personal favorite and I think it would be great for tuna salad or your chicken salad. If you like it, I can make more."

"Oooh, that sounds like it has a great crunch." Norm's eyes brightened at the idea of trying something new. Since he took over as the head chef at the bistro, the food was never boring and the customers were getting used to trying different sauces and combinations. Mark wasn't sure Bud Mathes - Chrissy's dad and former owner of the restaurant - even knew what an aioli was. Now, even the stodgy old farmers were asking for Norm to "slap some of that fancy sauce on a burger" for them.

"Maybe tomorrow after lunch, I'll swing by and find out what you need so I can work on that in the evening?"

"Perfect. Pretty soon, you'll have a feel for it, like Margaret did. Until then, we'll stay in close contact."

"Thanks, Norm. Let me know if anything doesn't taste right or you want it tweaked - denser, sweeter, etc. It's no problem to customize it for you guys."

"I'm sure it will be great, but I'll keep it in mind." Norm waved off her concerns with one of his large hands. Chrissy came into the kitchen looking for Norm. When she saw Mark, she gave him a quick hug.

"Mark, I haven't seen you much! School's out for the summer, right?" His heart dropped at the mention of school. His mind immediately made the jump from school to investigation.

"Hey Chrissy. Yeah, it's been a while. I'm working with Luke again this summer, so keeping busy. Plus - you and Todd are all newlywed bliss and ugh." He pretended to gag and then laughed to let her know he was joking.

"I know, I know. He's been meaning to call you to hang out. You should come over for the Fourth of July. We want to have everybody out for a big picnic and fireworks and the works. I think Luke has his mind set on some huge commercial fireworks. You know how ornery he is. Charlotte apparently never lit fireworks as a kid, so he thinks it is his mission in life to introduce her." Chrissy turned her attention to Danielle. "Oh my, I'm being so rude. I'm sorry, Danielle. You definitely need to come, too. There are so many people you need to meet now that you live here!" Mark watched as Danielle shrank back from the attention. Chrissy could be a bit loud and excitable, and Danielle's wide eyes gave away her discomfort.

He spoke up. "Try not to scare her off, Chrissy. I'm hoping I can convince her to go with me."

Chrissy clapped her hands and let out a small squeal. "That would be so great!" She turned again to Danielle and spoke with a more measured tone. "Mark is amazing. And if you can put up with his constant Harry Potter references and cartoons, you really couldn't ask for a better friend."

Danielle smiled shyly, "Thanks for the warning. He's been a pretty great friend so far."

Chrissy, satisfied with that answer, turned to Norm. "There's a church van from Ohio out there stopping for an early dinner. Just a heads up." She disappeared back to the front of the bistro and Norm quickly said goodbye so he could stay on top of the unexpected rush.

"She quite..." Danielle never finished the thought and Mark smiled.

"Yeah. Chrissy can come on a bit strong. But I've never met someone so genuinely joyful. She and Todd haven't been together long; but they are perfect together. Plus, what she has done with the restaurant is pretty amazing. You'd never guess that eight months ago, this place was a rundown cafe with tired decor and a tired menu."

"Hmmm. Maybe I'll have to pick her brain about running a business. I feel like I have a million things to learn. And the bakery isn't really even my business."

"You'll learn. And maybe it will be someday." Mark could only hope she would decide not to leave. Would the bakery keep her there? Or would she want to go back to the big city? He would do everything he could to make sure she stayed. Tonight, he would show her the charms of small-town life.

Chapter 8

Dani locked up the bakery and made the two-minute drive back to Margaret's house. She took a shower, grateful for the chance to rinse out her hair. Her natural curls became a mess of frizz if washed too often. Growing up, she fought her curls to the point of tears. Her mom insisted on brushing out her tight curls, not knowing any better, since her own pale brown hair was straight and wispy. When Dani was nearly thirteen, she realized her hair was dramatically different from her mom's and far closer to her father's. The years since had been a journey in education and trial and error to find the products and routine that embraced her natural curls instead of trying to tame them. They were anything but tame now; though she often pushed them back from her face with a pretty headband. A colorful scarf usually tied them back while baking.

After a shower, she stood in a towel and considered her clothing choices for the evening. They were getting dinner, but where? Should she dress up or down? In the end, she grabbed her jean shorts from the bottom drawer and was digging through her tops when she came to the printed tees she had buried in the stack. Dani thought of Mark - his adorable quirky sense of humor and their shared love of cartoons and fantasy worlds. Before she could talk herself out of it, she chose a blue tank top with a Super Mario logo that said "There ain't no party like a Mario Party" and threw it on. When she saw it at a booth in the mall in San Francisco, she knew she had to have it.

Dani fixed a quick dinner for her aunt, who insisted she didn't need to stick around. After making sure Aunt Maggie had everything she could need, Dani grabbed her phone and stuck her wallet in her back pocket. The warm air welcomed her as she opened the door to sit in the shade on the front steps.

A small, silver car drove up and Danielle stood. Mark got out and jogged up the walk. Salmon colored shorts fell above his knee paired with a patterned short-sleeve button down. He looked like he had stepped off the page of a magazine, and most definitely not like he belonged in this small Indiana town. Danielle thought he would fit in better in San Francisco with style. The other men she had seen around town were all in loose jeans or baggy cargo shorts. Mark's clothing was effortlessly stylish and complemented the carefully groomed stubble he'd had since she met him last week. Her heart stuttered. Skip, skip.

Oh man, I bet the sixth-grade girls positively obsess over him. She could imagine, remembering her own hopeless crushes as a young girl. There was something dreamy about a college-aged camp counselor when surrounded by annoying thirteen-year-old boys. Danielle had no problem imagining herself as a twelve-year-old girl sitting in class and dreaming about her cute teacher. If her teacher had looked like Mark, that is, instead of the plump and short-tempered sixty-five-year-old Mrs. Hansen.

"You look great." Mark touched her upper arms and leaned in to kiss her cheek. Skip, skip.

"Thanks," she managed. "You do too. I didn't really know what to expect." She let her voice trail off, asking if what she was wearing was appropriate with her hands gesturing to her outfit.

"It's perfect. We aren't going anywhere fancy." He gave her a reassuring smile and walked with her around the front of the car and opened her door. Skip, Skip. *I am in so much trouble. Friends. Friends. Just friends.* Mark had the air on full blast and the car felt cool, despite the ninety-degree weather lingering at seven in the evening.

Mark trotted around the back of the car to his seat. When he climbed in, he lowered the radio volume and turned to her. "Ready?"

"It's dangerous business, going out one's door." The quote from Lord of the Rings slipped out unbidden, and she hoped he would recognize it.

After a moment, he replied with the rest of the quote in a quiet, serious voice. "There's no knowing where you might be swept off to." She wondered if he was thinking what she was: it would be far too easy to be swept off her feet.

*****

Mark drove for twenty minutes before pulling onto a dead-end road and parking near a grove of trees.

Danielle looked around. "I guess a restaurant is not in the plans tonight?"

"Not tonight. But it will be worth it." Mark gave her a reassuring smile.

Only slightly concerned that she was in the middle of nowhere with someone she met only five days ago, she got out of the car and followed Mark through the trees. They emerged on the bank of a small river. He set a picnic basket she hadn't noticed he grabbed from the car on a weathered picnic table.

Then, Mark unloaded two folding chairs from their carrying cases and set them up.

"I'll be right back." He jogged back into the trees and Danielle sat down in a chair. She listened to the water flow quietly and heard Mark walking towards her through the trees. Loud footsteps and rustling grass interrupted the stillness.

He carried a grocery bag and an armful of split logs. Only then did Danielle notice the small ring of rocks in the ground in front of her.

Mark set the bag next to his chair and sat down. "You're from the city, right?" She confirmed with a nod. "Alright. Well, tonight you get to experience a good old-fashioned Indiana summer night. I've got hotdogs and s'mores to cook on the fire. Even better than that, we've got a river and the sky should be clear."

"Hotdogs?" Dani felt the gag in the back of her throat and swallowed it down. Anything but hotdogs. Well, anything but meat.

Mark smiled proudly. "Yep! It doesn't get more summery than hotdogs and s'mores."

Danielle tried to smile. She watched as Mark got the fire started. He grabbed the picnic basket and began to rifle through it. Chips, fruit, and bottles of root beer appeared from the woven wooden container. Then, the dreaded hotdogs. Dani looked away. *I have to tell him.*

"Here you go." He extended a hotdog speared

on a wire stick, handle first.

She shook her head. "I'm okay for now." She was still trying to fight the thick feeling of her stomach trying to crawl up her throat. Don't hurl, Dani. She munched on chips and tried to distract herself.

Mark held the hotdog over the fire and rotated it slowly. "Are you sure you don't want it? I'll even cook it for you, since you are an amateur and all," he joked while looking at the fire. He looked back at her and she saw the laughter in his eyes fade to concern. "Are you okay? You look like you might be sick."

Dani eyed the hotdog and resisted the urge to scoot away from it. "I'm actually a vegetarian." At the bistro, she'd watched him eat a chicken sandwich without issue, but she'd seen a documentary once that talked about hotdogs. Years later, it still made her squeamish.

With wide eyes, Mark apologized. "I'm sorry, I never even considered - I mean, we don't get too many vegetarians around here. This was a bad idea. We can go somewhere else. I can get you something." He pulled his stick out of the fire.

Flooded with the possibility of the night ending too soon, she babbled. "No, no. I want to stay. I just don't want a hotdog. Or to see a hotdog at all, actually." An uncomfortable laugh escaped with her admission.

He glanced at his stick and looked back at her. "Give me a minute." Then, he went behind her somewhere and returned with no offending food in sight. Mark gave her the bowl of watermelon pieces and they took turns eating the fruit with their fingers.

"Want to know a funny story?" She asked him after she'd relaxed.

"Of course." Mark popped a piece of watermelon into his mouth, and the juice ran down his chin before he swiped it with a paper towel.

"When I first went to culinary school, I actually intended to be a full chef. I was getting ready for class one day and opened the walk-in fridge to get my vegetables for the day - I think we were working on sauces or something. And I walk into the cooler and there, like twelve inches in front of my face was a giant hog."

She heard Mark's gasp of laughter and expanded on the drama. "The entire thing, just hanging there with no skin or anything. Legs and ribcage - the whole shebang. I had to duck around it to get my food!" He was laughing now, and she was too. "When my heart stopped racing and my stomach settled, I asked the instructor about it. Apparently, you had to take butchering to be a chef and the upper level class would be doing pork that day. In that moment, I decided pastry chef was my calling. Not general chef."

"Well, that sounds horrifying." Mark added, still grinning.

"It definitely was. And I wasn't even a vegetarian at that point! But it was traumatic enough to push me in that direction." The sky was growing darker now, and the fire was low, the cracking of the wood mixing with the whisper of the creek. The heat of the day was dissipating and Danielle rubbed her shoulders. Bugs were buzzing around her arms and she felt the sting of one before she could wipe it away.

After a moment, Mark's warm voice responded. "I became a teacher because I wanted to show kids it was okay to embrace yourself. Not sure if you noticed, but I'm not exactly your typical country boy."

"I don't know. Your campfire building skills are pretty solid." She smiled at him. "But, yeah. I understand."

"Growing up here wasn't always easy. Guys in high school weren't into Lord of the Rings or the latest Dune novel. It was football and girls and reality television." He gave an exaggerated shudder. "It took me a long time to be okay with being weird. And if I can be the one adult in a kid's life that lets him know that he can be whoever God created him to be, then that's what I want to do. I wish I would have had that." He shrugged, "Plus, it's pretty fun to teach those little weirdos. They are hilarious.

Infuriating," he added with raised eyebrows, "but hilarious."

Danielle laughed and slapped at a mosquito. Stupid bugs.

"Oh, crud. I forgot I brought bug spray. Hopefully it's not too late." Mark pulled a green can out of the grocery bag and handed it to her. Dani sprayed it on, wrinkling her nose at the chemical smell. If it meant the night didn't have to end, she'd tolerate it. She passed the can back to him and raised an eyebrow when he didn't put any on. He gave her a sheepish smile. "I put some on before I picked you up."

"Oh sure, leave me out here as some sort of all-you-can-eat mosquito buffet!" Danielle joked with him.

Mark hung his head in defeat. "I'm sorry, Dani. First the food and now this! I'll be lucky if you don't take the first flight back to San Francisco at this rate."

She smiled. "It hasn't been that bad. But I'll probably be willing to stay out later if you have an extra jacket or something." There was a chill in the wind now that the sun had gone down and the heat from the fire was nearly nonexistent.

"Be right back." Mark jogged back into the woods, leaving her in the dark. She tilted her head back and rubbed her arms and thighs while she studied the sky.

"Wow," she whispered to herself. Stars like this didn't exist in the city. There were thousands! A blinking red light move across the sky.

"Here you go." She jumped at Mark's voice behind her. She grabbed the blanket and wrapped it around her shoulders and over her bare legs.

"Look!" she said. "Do you see that red light? What do you think it is?"

Mark laid another log on the fire and took his seat after moving it slightly closer to hers. He looked toward where she pointed. "Probably an airplane. They have red lights. Look, there is another one where you can see both wings." Sure enough, she spotted a plane in another part of the sky.

"I've never seen so many stars in my entire life," Dani admitted.

"Isn't it amazing? I love coming out here to admire the universe. Makes you realize how big God is, doesn't it?" Big didn't even begin to cover it. Life had revealed God to be bigger and more faithful than she could imagine. Not even looking at a million stars on display as a show of His glory. But it was a start.

She tried to nod, her head still tipped back and looking at the dark sky. Moments passed in comfortable silence. "Do you think we'll see a shooting star?"

Mark paused. "Maybe. There are meteor

showers this fall, for sure. But you can look for satellites instead," he offered.

"Really?"

"Sure, give me a second." He looked at the sky and she tried to figure out what a satellite would look like. Maybe it was that bright one. "Satellite!" he pointed, and she tried to locate it. "It's moving pretty fast left to right and will pass by that really bright star in three, two, one, now!"

She smiled broadly when she found it. "Whoa!" She watched the tiny speck of light move across the sky, zooming by stars and eventually disappearing into the horizon.

"There's another one. It's a lot slower."

"What? Where?" Her eyes danced across the sky, trying to find the tiny light.

Mark pointed again, but she couldn't find it. "Sorry, it's gone. Maybe you can find the next one."

Dani studied, determined to find one. She spotted several airplanes, and her eyes caught faster movement. There! "Got it! It's around the same path as the first one was taking."

"Nice!"

Danielle soaked in the peaceful moment. The fire was alive again, devouring the log Mark had added, and the water in the creek still lapped at the rocks on the edge. She heard the hum of bugs and the very distant sound of tires on pavement. She looked out across the creek to the field on the other side. "What are all those little lights?"

She looked at Mark and his eyes were wide. "You're kidding."

"What? Are they fireflies? I've always wanted to catch one."

Mark chuckled. "Around here, we call them lightning bugs. But yeah. Those are them."

"Can we catch one?" She knew it sounded childish. But catching a firefly was something she'd always heard about. California didn't have them, at least not in the city.

He laughed louder. "Of course, we can." Mark stood and held a hand out to her. She left the blanket on her chair and followed him away from the light of the fire. It didn't take long before she could see the black bugs, even when they weren't illuminated. "Stand still," Mark instructed. He stood next to her and they waited. Then, he whispered in her ear. "Cup your hands and wait until one gets close."

He cupped his own hands in demonstration. He took one step forward and his hands closed around a glowing yellow bug. He brought it back to her and opened his hands. She laughed as the bug emerged and came toward her face. "Okay, okay. My turn."

She spotted a lightning bug and reached out toward it but missed. Then, she missed again. Mark said nothing, and she was grateful for his silence. She spotted the slow flash of a bug coming toward her from the left. She held her hands open and crossed the distance with two steps before cupping her hands gently around the insect. It bumped around her palm and she opened her hands just enough to peek inside and watch the 'lightning bug' illuminate the tiny cave.

She turned to look at Mark with a wide smile. "So cool."

Mark returned her smile. "It's really fun to hit them on the highway while they are lit up. The guts keep glowing on your windshield for about ten seconds after they die."

She gasped and freed the bug from her hands. She turned to him with an open mouth and a choked laugh. "That's awful!"

He laughed in return and wrapped his arms around her. "I'm just kidding. I mean, it is kind of cool, but I don't particularly enjoy knowing that I killed a harmless bug." He looked down at her, his slightly taller frame giving him a height advantage.

Her breath caught and she ducked her head. "Thanks for teaching me how to catch fireflies."

"They are called lightning bugs. And you're welcome." He released her and she exhaled deeply as she walked back to her waiting camp chair, rubbing her arms. It wasn't the chill this time. It was permanent imprint of his arms around her.

Mark sat down beside her after poking at the fire. With a smile on her face, she looked again at

the impossible number of stars. A peace settled
deep in her heart as she spoke into the silence again
and pointed up, "Satellite."

Chapter 9

Mark woke up in the morning and spotted the almost full package of hotdogs in his fridge. *Vegetarian, of course. Why didn't I notice. Or ask?* He continued kicking himself for the mistakes of the evening before. He grabbed a cold hot dog and called it breakfast while he smiled at the memory of catching lightning bugs with Danielle. He couldn't believe she'd never seen one before, they seemed so common in his world. He remembered capturing them by the dozen as a kid and keeping them in mason jars with hole-punched lids. As with everything else, it had been a competition between him and his brothers. Who could get the most? Usually, it wasn't him. Malachi and Daniel were competitive. It was a good thing they'd had different interests. Daniel being the jock and Malachi being the brains was probably the saving grace of their tiny house. If the two of them had competed directly? It would have combusted.

Spending the day with Danielle had been exactly what Mark needed to get his mind off the accusations and the investigation. But today was Monday again and he had nothing to look forward to but manual labor and serious time with his headphones. No lawns to mow today; he would be redoing some of the display landscapes in front of Luke's office and supply yard. Apparently, they'd been the same for too long and Luke thought they needed switched up. Luke wasn't completely selfish and would be working alongside Mark on the project. Which was exactly what Mark didn't want.

Could he hide the issue that was eating at him from someone who knew him well? Danielle didn't know better, so if he was quieter than usual or let a sarcastic comment slip; she had no baseline for normal. But Luke or Todd? They knew him. Like, *really* knew him. He wanted to keep this hidden though. There was no telling what people would think, and even though Luke wasn't just 'people'... Mark cared what he thought. The idea that his friends might doubt him, even for a minute, made him want to throw up the cold hotdog he already regretted eating.

He said a quick prayer that he could keep up the

act, knowing that it wasn't the right thing to pray for. But he didn't care at this point. His entire drive, all four minutes of it, to work, he lectured himself and gave himself his own weak excuses. *You should be telling people so they can surround the investigation with prayer. But then people will know. You only look more guilty for hiding this. I'll be cleared and no one will ever know. You need someone to carry this burden with you. I can do this myself. It'll be over soon.*

He decided there was no point in arguing with himself, because he always won. Or lost. Whichever way you wanted to look at it. Today he was doing nothing except working. He reached to grab his headphones from their normal spot on the passenger seat and then let out a groan. In his eager preparations for dinner with Danielle last night, he'd cleaned out his car and carried his headphones inside. He'd have to make it through this entire day working beside Luke without even the shield of music or podcasts to avoid conversation. *Are you kidding me, God?*

Carry each other's burdens.

I would happily carry someone else's burden. Yes, let's go with that. Maybe Luke has something he needs to share?

He got no answer. Debating with God was even less fruitful than debating with himself. He pulled his hat down and climbed out of his car. The morning was already steamy and the air was thick. It was going to top a hundred degrees today. Luke wouldn't have them working on the project during the heat of the day, but Mark knew he'd want to knock most of it out before lunch, despite the warm morning.

"Mornin'!" Luke waved a dirty hand and greeted him across the parking lot. He had already pulled out half of the retaining wall stones and was creating a new wall about fifteen feet away, on the opposite side of the front office door.

"Hey. You got a plan for this?"

"Yep. I want to move these and create a tiered look. And I'm going to hook up a fountain, too. That's the big change."

"Flagstone?"

"Exactly. Sort of like the one we did out in front of the barn at Bloom's Farm. But enough people see that one, I want to make this one unique. Any ideas?"

"I'll think about it while we tear this out." Mark was grateful Luke was eager to get to work and didn't make small talk. Hopefully that continued later into the day.

*****

Two hours later, Luke and Mark sat on a carefully constructed ledge of landscaping stones.

Both men were sweaty and had dirt smudged on their face where they had swiped at beads of sweat with dirty forearms. Mark gulped from the straw on the red, one-gallon drink cooler he brought with him each day. It couldn't be further from the small, metal water bottle he used at school and filled up as needed between classes. Each year he bought a new one, and last year's container had a Batman logo on it. Today's cooler was plain, unadorned and designed for one purpose - carry a lot of water and keep it cold. Luke sat beside him, rubbing his forehead with a towel before replacing his grungy baseball hat. Salt stains created mountain landscapes on the hat, evidence of days even sweatier than this one.

Luke studied the ground, playing with the towel. "Charlotte and I are trying to have a baby."

"Whoa, man. That's awesome! I didn't know you guys wanted kids so soon." Mark looked at his friend and tried to read his expression and body language.

"Yeah. Thanks. I wasn't sure I would want any at all after Rachel and the baby. But the idea of having one with Charlotte?" He smiled and looked up at Mark. "I'm ready, you know?"

Mark grinned. Luke had been devastated when his first wife died, carrying their unborn child. "Of course, you are. You and Charlotte will be awesome parents."

"I don't know. Neither of us have the best example to follow."

"And that sucks. But you've got better examples to follow. You've got Miss Ruth. And you've got a perfect heavenly Father. Plus, you know what not to do, that's for sure." Both Luke and Charlotte had a less-than-idea upbringing, to say the least.

"Hah, I suppose we do." Luke drank deeply from his own large water cooler. "I'm just scared. Afraid I won't be good at it."

"There is nothing to worry about. Charlotte will kick you out of your grumpy moods, and if you love your baby half as much as you love her - that will be one lucky kid."

Luke laughed. "Thanks, Mark. It feels good to tell someone. No success yet, but it's not for lack of trying!"

Mark set down his cooler and covered his ears and began to chant, "La, la, la. I can't hear you!" He cracked up and Luke gave him a jab on the shoulder.

Luke changed the subject, turning to Mark. "What's up with you? School year finish up okay?"

Mark tried to keep the smile pasted on his face. Here was an opening. Should he tell Luke? Could he? "Yep. All good. Nothing real exciting in my world."

"What about the new girl in town?" Mark gave him a quizzical look and Luke explained. "Don't act surprised that Chrissy said something to Charlotte."

"And of course, Charlotte mentioned it to you." Mark rolled his eyes and Luke shrugged in response. "It's no big deal. She's new in town, and I don't think she'll be here long. I guess we kind of hit it off. She's cute and hilarious and get this: she knows comic books."

"You are telling me your dream girl moves to town and it is no big deal?" Luke used finger quotes around the last three words.

Mark felt the heat rise in his cheeks, even though it was already pushing ninety degrees. "She might not even stick around. I'm just trying to be a friend. She doesn't know anybody, okay?"

"Sure, sure. Remember, Charlotte wasn't going to stick around, either."

Mark thought about that. He remembered meeting Charlotte. Her city clothes and car had stuck out like Spiderman at a wedding. Perhaps a bit like him and his more unusual style. But he was a native and people let him get away with it. Everything about Charlotte had screamed that she wouldn't stick around Minden for the long term. But by Thanksgiving, she belonged as well as anyone. She still wore high heels most days, but she seemed happy here. Luke had a lot to do with it, judging by how in love they were. Could Danielle live here permanently? With him? She had family here. It seemed like she and Margaret were getting along, even though it had been years since they'd last seen each other.

There was too much up in the air. He barely knew her. And there was a lot she didn't know about him. How could he think about whether she would stay in Minden when he didn't know for sure if he would be able to stay. He couldn't shake the fear that the accusations would blow up and he would have to leave.

"There's something else." Mark caught Luke's glance and took a deep breath. "You remember that meeting last week when I had to cut my day short to run over to the admin office?" Luke nodded. "I thought it was something small, but it ended up being serious."

Wrinkles appeared between Luke's eyebrows as he asked, "What's up?"

"Apparently there is some student claiming that I-" Mark broke off, choking on the words. Disgusting, infuriating words describing something even more vile and appalling. "That I touched them. Inappropriately." Mark pressed his eyes shut and hung his head, ashamed even to admit the words.

Luke sucked in a breath and then exhaled the words, "Geez, Mark." Mark looked up at his friend, afraid of what he would see. There was no disgust in Luke's eyes. He saw eyes wide with disbelief soften with pain. "I mean, that's the most ridiculous thing I've ever heard. Anybody that knows you even a little realizes that it has to be false. But why didn't you say anything?"

"I couldn't! Don't you get it? Even though it isn't true, I'll always be the teacher who might have abused a student! I can't be that person. People already think I'm weird because I wear skinny jeans, for crying out loud. I'll be run out of town. I've seen it before!" Mark was getting riled up now. He stood up and began to pace in front of Luke's place on the ledge. "Even after being found innocent, there are male teachers who can never get another job or have to move halfway across the country to teach again."

"Come on, that's not going to happen to you, Mark. You and your family are a staple in this community. No one is going to believe you did this."

He stopped pacing and looked at Luke for a long moment. "But...what if they do?" The words emerged shakily and he waited for an answer.

"Then, you'll stand by your innocence and you'll remember that they can't judge you."

Mark let out a shuddering breath and sat down heavily on the stones. "I don't know what to do, Luke. It's completely out of my control. What am I supposed to do? It's like I'm sitting in the waiting room, expecting test results confirming a terminal diagnosis."

"Come on, man. You've got to trust that the

investigation will clear you. You didn't do anything wrong, right?"

"Seriously, Luke?" His pulse raced at the question and his fists clenched.

"I want to hear you say it. Did you do anything wrong? Or that someone could misconstrue as inappropriate?"

"No. I haven't done anything." He let out a breath and unflexed his hands.

"Then leave it up to God. He's got your back." Luke stood up and laid a heavy hand on Mark's shoulder. "It's going to be fine. Let's pray about it before we get back to work, okay?"

Without waiting for permission and with his hand still on Mark's shoulder, Luke ducked his head. He prayed over the investigation and Mark's anxiety, right there on the edge of the parking lot, surrounded by dirt and rocks from the display. Mark relaxed into the words and he fought the sting of tears behind his eyes.

Carry one another's burdens.

I hear you, God. Thank you.

Chapter 10

Aunt Maggie insisted on coming into the bakery a week later, only a week after it was reopened. Dani brought out the cushioned office chair from the back and settled her aunt near one of the small tables in the front. From there, she held court most of the day. Dozens of people came in to see her once word spread that she was at the shop. Plus, nearly everyone who came purchased something.

During one of the lulls, Dani asked her Aunt, "Do you usually get this much traffic in the morning?"

"No, not usually. Sometimes people come in, but most of my foot traffic is at lunch or later."

"Oh good. I think if we were this busy all the

time, you would need someone running the register and counter all day so you could actually get some baking done."

Danielle's generous supply of cookies and cupcakes was disappearing, and she retrieved some cookie dough she'd frozen and threw it in the oven. The patience to decorate the intricate sugar cookies The Rolling Pin was known for eluded her. The cookies she made were delicious and, in the end, that was the most important part. Most people didn't stick around to eat. Aunt Maggie said it used to be more common, but with the renovation to the cafe and since Chrissy had started stocking goods from the Rolling Pin, more people were getting their cookie with a 'fancy coffee' from next door.

Danielle gathered Margaret wasn't a fan of the espresso machine and the complicated lattes and cappuccinos offered.

"Give me plain old coffee with milk and sugar any day," she said. It made things simple for Dani, though. She didn't have to worry about clearing dishes or refilling coffee cups. Maggie walked her through brewing a pot in the ancient coffee maker.

Aunt Maggie continued, "I have to say, though. If we could get people in the door for something special in the morning, we might sell more of the other treats. But I just don't know what we could do that Chrissy hasn't already taken care of."

Eager to consider the business-side of things,

Dani considered the options. B&J Bistro served a full breakfast and also had croissants and muffins provided by The Rolling Pin. "Any good donut places around here?" Maggie shook her head. "Bagels?" Another negative. "Neither would be too difficult, and might help increase your morning visitors. Not everyone wants a big breakfast. Plus, the bistro seems busy this morning. We could be a nice, quick alternative for people who just want a bite and a cup of 'plain old coffee'." She said the last part with a teasing wink.

Aunt Maggie laughed. "Speaking of plain old coffee; I'll take a refill."

"Coming right up. Just let me set out this butter for later." She grabbed the carafe and took it over to her aunt. "We will probably need to restock soon. Can you handle that part?"

Maggie shot her an annoyed glance. "Of course, I can. I'm injured, not brain dead. Just bring me my notebook from the desk. There is a stack of blank forms in the tray."

Danielle was grateful she wouldn't have to learn that process, yet. Yet? If she stuck around, she'd have to learn it, eventually. Was she considering staying? It was surprisingly fun to be here with her aunt.

Margaret took a sip of her coffee. "Ahhh. Tell you what, all I need is Jesus and a good cup of coffee." Danielle stopped in her tracks on her way back to the kitchen, nearly letting the coffee pot slip from her fingers.

"What did you say?"

"Oh, just something my mama used to say. Your grandma used to enjoy her first drink of coffee like it was a religious experience." Maggie chuckled. "All I need is Jesus and a good cup of coffee, she'd say."

Dani turned slowly and her voice was quiet. "Mom used to say that, too." It made sense, Margaret was her sister, but to hear Aunt Maggie say the same words she'd heard her mother whisper a hundred times? It brought a fresh slice of pain. "I miss her so much sometimes."

Margaret looked at her with wet eyes. "Oh sweetie. I do, too. I wish... I wish we could have moved on."

"From what? What was so terrible that she never came back here? That I couldn't grow up really knowing my grandparents?"

"Have a seat, Dani. This isn't really my story to tell, but you deserve to know. And since your mama's gone now," Maggie's voice thickened. She cleared her throat and blinked twice. "I guess it's my job. Beatrice and I... We were only four years apart in age, you know? Sometimes that felt like decades, but other times? We were thick as thieves. We ran around Minden, climbing trees and chasing boys. Your mama was beautiful. Just like you. Her long hair hung to her waist, and she was athletic and oh-so-happy. I, on the other hand, was always kind of chubby. The same hair that looked so luscious on her seemed stringy and oily on me. I was jealous most of the time even though she was younger than me. We fought and made up and fought again.

"When she was eighteen, I was twenty -two. She was the bane of my existence. It was hard to look cool to the older boys when your sister is always tagging along. She always got more of their attention, despite being younger. But our parents always made me include her. Oh boy, I hated that." Maggie chuckled. "It wasn't her fault. Really, it wasn't mine either, now that I look back. I was so frustrated that our parents gave her so much more freedom than they had ever given me. As much freedom and independence as they gave her, she always wanted more. But by the time she was old enough, she wanted nothing more than to get out of Minden. So, she did."

"She went to California. For a while, she sent back postcards and letters. Occasionally, the house phone would ring and we would pass it around to talk with her until she ran out of quarters for the payphone.

" Maggie smiled at the memory, staring into her coffee mug. "About six years after she left, she finally came home. With a man." Aunt Maggie shook her head. "I thought our father would have a heart attack. There was an ugly scene in the front yard, Bea standing between the two of them." Her aunt looked at Dani and grabbed her hand across the small table. "Grandpa missed out on something amazing in knowing you by not accepting your daddy. And none of that is your fault, okay, sweetie?"

Dani couldn't bring herself to respond. The new information seeped into her memory, trying to connect the dots of overheard conversations and missing relatives. "Our mother was too timid to stand up to him. She couldn't bring herself to welcome Beatrice home, when my father was so offended and upset. And I'm sorry to say, I was too. Bea and I stayed in touch through letters after that. When you were born, she sent me pictures. And you remember when I came out to see you?"

Dani stared at the wall behind her aunt, as though she could see into the past. She remembered that visit. Remembered mixing up cookies while standing on a chair at the kitchen table. There was laughter. and the taste of chocolate chips on her tongue as she stole a spoonful of cookie dough. Confused at the single happy memory, she moved her gaze back to her aunt. "What happened? Why didn't you ever come back?"

Maggie pressed her lips together. "I let my own prejudices get in the way." Shaking her head, she leaned across the table. "I could see how much Bea

loved your daddy, but I had all the horrible things
my father still believed rattling around my head.
The things he would comment while watching the
news. Your dad had just been laid off. Lots of
people were around that time," Aunt Maggie leaned
back, as though hesitant to admit the rest, "But I
said some awful things, Dani. And your mama sent
me away."

She closed her eyes and continued, "She said by
not accepting him, I was rejecting you. And her.
And she was right." Dani saw the sorrow in
Maggie's wrinkled face, and saw the wetness shine
when she opened her eyes. "He's a good man. And I
couldn't see it then. I'm so sorry, sweetie. I wish I
could take it back. Since then, God has showed me
over and over again how every person is in His
image."

Dani stared blankly, refusing to acknowledge
the regret in her aunt's eyes. "I don't understand.
You came to see us and you still couldn't get over
the fact that my dad was black? What did you say
that would make her so upset?"

Margaret shook her head, denying Danielle's
curiosity. "It doesn't matter anymore, Danielle. It
was ignorance talking, and I'd take it back if I
could. But by the time I realized how wrong I was,
it had been years. I sent a few letters, but I never
had the courage to go back out to California and see
her in person." Margaret's tears were spilling over

114

now, and she dabbed them with a napkin. "Beatrice never forgave me. Not that I blame her. And now it's too late. I can't believe she's gone. Maybe it's not too late for me to make things right with your father. I owe him the apology, even more than I owed one to Bea."

"Well, it's too late for that, too." Dani stood, pacing. "He was killed in a car accident when I was eleven. Mom was devastated. I don't think she ever really got over it. She needed her sister and you weren't there!" Dani was yelling, but despite Maggie's flinching, she couldn't stop.

Margaret closed her eyes for a moment and let out a breath. "Oh, Dani. I'm so sorry you had to go through that, I hope you can forgive me." She pleaded with Dani. "Honestly, I never imagined I would get the chance to make things right with you. I loved you from the minute I saw you. Since I saw your mom's eyes on your tiny face. I didn't see you as black. You were just family."

"But I *am* black. I always will be! Just because I'm not as dark as my father, you loved me? But not him? That's not even possible. If you had really loved me, you would have accepted my father."

Margaret wiped her eyes and let out a sigh. "You're probably right, you know. I thought I loved you back then. In reality, I could love the part of you that was like me. Like my sister. But Dani - can you believe me when I say now that I love every part of you? That if your father were here now, I'd make him a cup of coffee and we could talk together about how wonderful you are? I let my father's flawed beliefs and my own inexperience ruin the chance to know the man my sister loved. That's my loss."

"You're right. It is your loss." Dani had to get away. She escaped behind the counter and into the walk-in fridge of the bakery. She took deep breaths of the cool air and tried to calm her racing heart. Her throat was raw and hot at the realization that her only remaining family had rejected her all those years ago. It didn't matter that Aunt Maggie had apparently 'looked past' the part of her that was black. *Oh great, at least my Aunt was able to get over the fact that I was half black,* she let the sarcastic thought echo bitterly in her mind. She shook her head and fought the tears that threatened. Here she was, hoping she could make a home here in Minden. Maybe it was too much. Maybe she was better off without a family at all. Better no family than one who thought only half of her identity was worth loving.

What did she have to go back to, though? Other than Casey and the girls at Knit Night - she didn't have any real friends in California. She had no money, no car, and no job. Plus, it was expensive to live out there. She realized just how expensive it was when she saw a for sale sign on a house with the price listed. For that much money in San Francisco, she couldn't buy a three-hundred-square-foot studio. And what about Mark? She'd definitely miss him if she left. And the bakery. She was having fun. Norm stopped by and said he loved her sunflower oat bread. She found she really enjoyed the challenges of doing more than cupcakes and sweet treats. Plus, if they started doing donuts or bagels a few times a week, she could work on those skills, too.

She didn't want to leave. As much as it hurt to hear Aunt Maggie admit that she had rejected Dani's father, she recalled their interactions since she arrived. It never seemed like Aunt Maggie saw her any differently. What was it she'd said? "Now, I love every part of you." Did she believe that? There had been too many people over the years who hadn't. There had been friends who mocked her love of Japanese cartoons and boyfriends who wanted her to straighten her curly hair. Not to mention the parents of boyfriends who gave no reason for their dislike. Or creepy hotel supervisors who insisted if she just smiled more and wore tighter clothes, she'd be an exotic beauty and sure to succeed. All of this said with his hand on her thigh. The memory brought stomach acid to her throat. With few exceptions, people in her life had always seen something that needed changing. Her skin was too dark for some. Too light for others. Her interests not feminine enough for some, not intellectual enough for others. Too much and not enough, all at once. Her small family had been the only ones who seemed to accept her exactly as she was. Could she give up on the only family she had left?

She straightened her shoulders and sent up a quick prayer. *Help me see Aunt Maggie's heart like you do, God. Help me forgive her and show grace. I'm not sure I can do it without you at this point.*

With that, she walked back into the kitchen and got to the work she'd been neglecting while Aunt Maggie told her story. There would be time to talk more later, but for now, she had a princess cake to make. And a lot of family history to emotionally unpack.

Chapter 11

Unloading on Luke was good for Mark. It was nice to not have to keep the secret to himself. This weekend, he was excited to head to Indianapolis for the gaming convention he attended each year. He loved to visit the booths to talk to artists, actors, and game creators. His favorite part was seeing the people that created elaborate costumes of popular characters. Mark messaged with some of his online friends from Indianapolis and tracked down an extra ticket. Eagerly, he texted Danielle.

MD: Comic-con is this week in Indy. Do you think you can get away?

DW: Seriously? I haven't
been to a con in years.
I'm in.

MD: Awesome. I'll pick you
up at 7 AM Saturday.

DW: Do you have a
costume?

MD: Not this year.

DW: Phew. Maybe next
time.

Mark grinned at the insinuation. Usually, he
rolled his eyes at the couples he saw at the
convention in their coordinating costumes. Prince
and princess. Leia and Luke from Star Wars.
Batman and Catwoman. If he was being honest, he
was envious they found someone they shared those
interests with. The possibility that he and Danielle
could make matching costumes for the next
convention sent jitters through his stomach. Would
he still be around next year?

When Saturday morning arrived, Mark woke
before his alarm and had to restrain himself from
arriving at Margaret's house too early. Just like
when he picked her up for dinner, Danielle was

sitting on the step. When she stood up, his laughter boomed across the yard. She had on jeans and a printed shirt that said "Boom Spock a Locka" with a picture of Spock from Star Trek. She looked down and smiled.

"I love it," he said with amusement.

Dani shrugged. "Can't go wrong with Star Trek at a con, right?"

"It's only logical," he joked in a poor impersonation of Spock. She giggled and his smiled widened. "Should we hit the road? The convention will be in full swing when we get there. Some of my friends are saving seats for us at the Avengers panel."

Danielle thrust a small, soft object into his hands. "Here, this is for you." When he spun it around and looked at it, he realized it was a stuffed insect. "It turned out looking more like a bee than I wanted. So, I put this lightning bolt on the yellow part."

"Holy smokes. Did you make this? It's a lightning bug?" he confirmed. She nodded. "That's so cool. I love it, Dani. How did you make it? Is it knitted?" Mark fingered the wings, amazed at how they stood away from the body.

"It's crochet. It's called amigurumi. I wanted to make something to remember the other night. And I made myself one, too." She turned her smile toward him and the full force of her warm topaz eyes hit him. He couldn't say anything, too touched by the gift and entranced by her gaze. And he couldn't look away. Mark definitely didn't need any help to remember that night. The small stuffed animal was the most unique, thoughtful give he'd ever received.

"Wow. I'm... Thanks, Danielle." Mark gave her a quick hug, her sweet coconut scent surrounding him for an all-too-brief moment. Once they were in the car, he set the baseball-sized insect in a cubby on the dash, next to the clock display.

At the convention, he noticed the glances Danielle received walking around the center. The show had about three times as many guys as girls, and she definitely stood out, even among the women in attendance. Mark watched as she found a booth at the convention selling dozens of stuffed animals, similar to what she created. He'd never noticed a booth like that before, but presumably they'd always been there. Danielle chatted with the woman manning the booth, and he stared as she tipped her head back and laugh. He let himself get lost in watching her. She was magnificent, and she was here with him. It still amazed him.

Danielle sat through hours of interviews and stood in lines to meet actors from his favorite TV show. All without a complaint. In fact, she seemed to enjoy it as much as he did. She'd actually squealed with excitement when she spotted the booth for an obscure Japanese cartoon he barely recognized.

Then, she browsed a booth with hundreds of printed T-shirts and snapped pictures of her favorites. Dani didn't buy anything though. He'd already bought a poster, two books, and a new water bottle for the next school year with the Flash on it.

"Don't you want to get one?" Mark gestured to the T-shirts, where she'd been looking at a Spiderman shirt that said, "I was on the web before it was cool."

Danielle just shook her head. "I'm good."

"Okay," he relented. But when they split up so they could attend different presentations, he doubled back and picked out a shirt for her. It said, "Come to the dark side, we have cupcakes." It had a picture of Darth Vader holding a cupcake and made him think of her. By the end of the day, they were both knackered. They climbed into his car, and the trapped air, hot and thick, covered them like a blanket.

"That was awesome, Mark. Thanks for inviting me."

"I'm really glad you were able to come. I wouldn't have enjoyed it nearly as much without you." He admitted. "To mark the occasion, I got you something."

Danielle turned to him with wide eyes. "What? You already paid for my ticket to the con!"

"Well, if you don't want it..." He pulled the plastic bag he was offering back toward himself.

"I didn't say I didn't want it!" She reached out and opened and closed her hands twice. "Gimme, gimme."

"I noticed you like funny shirts, so..."

"Boom spock a locka!" she said with laughter in her voice. Dani pushed her hands toward the ceiling in a goofy dance. His heart danced in time with her wacky moves. She's perfect.
Mark held up the Star Wars themed shirt so she could read it and was pleased when she grabbed it with a smile and a laugh. "Oh my gosh, it's incredible!"

"I thought so." He watched her rub the shirt against her cheek and relished her genuine excitement. Today had shown him a playful side of Danielle, one as offbeat and unconventional as his own.

"I love it. I never really imagined I'd find a guy who wasn't turned off by my strange obsession with movies and games. Lots of guys say they want a girl into video games, but they don't actually want her to know things."

"Yeah. I've seen the same thing. Around here it's usually guy who claim they want a woman into sports. But when she can breakdown the offensive scheme and talk circles around him about the most recent trade deal; it's suddenly not so attractive. I never wanted a girlfriend who simply tolerates my wanting to play board games, but someone who actually wants to play with me."

She set the shirt on her lap and turned toward him. "Oh, yes! What board games?"

And they were off on a discussion of board games from around the world. It lasted until they saw the glow of the QuikStop on the side of the highway, marking their return to Minden. Mark pulled into Margaret's driveway and walked around to open the door for Danielle. Her hands were empty as she'd already put her new shirt on over her Spock one.

When she stepped out of the car, he reached around her and shut the door; stepping close. Mark's mouth went dry, and he desperately wanted to kiss her. Something was holding him back, though. The dark cloud of the accusations had lightened today, but returned in the quiet evening. Instead, he wrapped her in his arms and gave a slight squeeze. "Goodnight, Dani."

"Goodnight, Mark." She whispered over the sound of the insects in the trees.

After he retreated to his car, he released a breath from his cheeks and laid his forehead on the steering wheel.

Chapter 12

Aunt Maggie was getting more and more independent and mobile every day. She ditched her walker and replaced it with a wide-based cane. Danielle even caught her in the kitchen at the bakery a few times. When Dani realized that her Aunt was no better at sitting still than she was, she set up a cookie decorating station where Aunt Maggie could safely sit and pipe icing on the summer-themed sugar cookies everyone had been missing. This week's cookies were American flags and fireworks for the upcoming holiday. The temptation to remain upset with Maggie was still strong. It felt like she was dishonoring her father's memory to be living with the woman who thought so little of him. A simple look in the mirror was all it took to remind her of their differences. Too much and not enough. With every small reminder of her mother in the house, she wondered if Beatrice would have forgiven Maggie, eventually.

Was she weak, latching on to an aunt who rejected her so many years before? Was she so desperate for a family that she wouldn't stand up for her father and her heritage? Dani didn't want to be angry. It did no good to dwell on the ugliness of people. There was too much hate in the world. In the country. Much of it centered on race. As much as she wanted it not to matter, it did. And Aunt Maggie: as much as she wanted her cruel words to have never been spoken; they were. Those words caused a rift with her sister that would never be repaired. And Danielle was faced with the choice. Could she put the past behind her and let Maggie's actions today determine their future? The emotional whiplash was exhausting. The only bright spot was running the bakery. And spending time with Mark.

Mark asked her to go to Chrissy and Todd's house for the day of the fourth. She had slowly gotten to know people in Minden. Luke and Charlotte invited them over for dinner, and Dani immediately bonded with Charlotte over crochet and the things they missed about city living. Dani was far more nervous about tonight. Mark had invited her for dinner at his parents' house.

After closing the bakery, she took a shower and changed into a soft purple sun dress. It was a far cry from the screen tees she had grown comfortable wearing around Mark and Maggie, but she wanted to dress up. She needed Mark's family to like her. What if they didn't approve? She probably wasn't what they had pictured as their son's girlfriend.

Danielle smoothed her dress for the twentieth time as they stood in front of his parents' house. "You are beautiful, Dani. Just relax. They will love you." As Mark reassured her, he knocked lightly and then opened the screen door. "*Marco?* Is that you!" She heard the loud voice before she saw the source turn the corner toward the entryway. "Ah, my favorite son! Especially today, because you brought this lovely young woman to meet me. How have I been a mother for thirty-five years and none of my sons have ever brought a girl home?" Without waiting for an answer, his mother pulled his head toward her and kissed the top. "Never mind that, she's here now." Donna Dawson opened her arms and embraced Danielle. His mom was soft and the scent of garlic danced around her. While she hugged Danielle, she spoke to Mark. "She's *molto bella*, Mark! You didn't tell me!" Danielle adored the way Mark's mother sprinkled accented Italian through her words. Aside from the Italian, her voice had a typical midwestern accent. "Call me Donna, sweetheart. I'm just so thrilled you are here. Come, come, into the kitchen. My friend Margaret tells me you can really bake!"

Dani gave Mark a helpless glance and trailed behind Donna, who still held on to one hand. Mark just raised his shoulders in a shrug.

"Mom! I'm home!" A voice called from the other room.

"Ah, that's Stephen. Have you met Stephen yet? Such a good boy. Of course, you can't go wrong with my *Marco*." Stephen came around the corner. He had similar coloring to Mark, dark hair and eyes against smooth, light skin. *So, this is Captain America.* "Stephen! I'm so glad you are here!" Donna greeted him with the same exuberant tone she had welcomed Mark.

"What? No favorite son tonight?" Stephen asked with a teasing tone.

"Did you bring home a girlfriend? *Non*? Then tonight you're the second favorite!" Stephen smiled and waved at Dani before spotting Mark in the other room and heading that way. Dani watched with interest. Donna seemed unconcerned that calling him her second favorite son would upset him. Donna leaned over as though telling her a secret. "All my boys are my favorite. All five of them, can you believe it?"

"I don't know how you did it, Mrs. Dawson."

"Call me Donna. Tell me about yourself, Danielle. I've seen you working while I catch up with Margaret; but we haven't had a chance to talk!"

Donna was full of energy and laughter, and the

way she spoke of each of her sons filled Dani with longing. What would it have been like to grow up surrounded by the raucous laughter coming from the other room? So different from the quiet evenings she spent with her parents, watching TV and reading. When she built a fort, it was with her dad. Dani imagined Mark and his brothers created their own adventures daily growing up. Based on the dates she'd been on with Mark, he was still that way. He planned the entire campfire outing and initiated the trip to Indianapolis. Of course, the other night they had simply stayed at her Aunt's house and watched a movie. Loki didn't like Mark, which she took to be a good sign, since Loki was the super-villain and hated the good guys.

Danielle helped Donna get dinner on the table and sat back during dinner, enjoying the exchanges between Mark and his brothers. Gideon had a job interview tomorrow and Mark tried to give him advice, which Gideon promptly rolled his eyes at. Mark's dad was unexpected. It shouldn't have surprised her, knowing that he had at least one brother who played in the NFL, but Richard's size was impressive. When he greeted her with a big hug, the top of her head barely reached his armpit. Gideon was similarly built.

When dinner ended, Mark's mom kicked everyone out to the backyard and they took turns cranking the handle of an old-fashioned ice cream maker. "Come on mom, can't we get an electric one like everyone else? Next thing you know, you'll have us churning our own butter." Gideon's whining during his turn to crank made Mark catch her eye and roll his. She made her way over to him, realizing she hadn't been next to Mark for most of the evening.

"He's young," she told him.

"Or I'm old."

"Maybe. But I think those gray hairs just make you look distinguished." Danielle ruffled the short hair above his ears, where lighter hairs were encroaching on the rich brown of the hair he could attribute to his Italian roots.

She watched his cheeks redden and she stood on her tiptoes to kiss his cheek. He wrapped his closer arm around her and held her next to him. "I'm glad you're here, Dani."

"Me too. Your family is pretty amazing."

"Dani! It's your turn!" Gideon yelled across the deck and other voices chimed in their protests.

"I don't think so!"

"She's our guest."

"Gideon Matthew, don't you dare!" Donna admonished him.

Danielle laughed at them. "Honestly, I'd love to take a turn. It will be another first for me."

Mark looked at her. "Okay, but let me know when your arm is tired." He leaned in and whispered in her ear, "I'll finish your shift."

About thirty seconds in, Danielle was thinking no ice cream could possibly taste good enough to warrant this kind of effort. A minute later and she had switched from left to right to left arm again.

"Done?" Mark gave her a knowing smile.

"Nope. Easy peasy," she lied. Gideon and Stephen were watching her. She thought she heard something about a bet, which fueled her determination.

After what seemed like an hour later, Donna shouted, "Whoop! Atta girl. She did a whole five minutes!"

"And wouldn't you know--she complained less than you, Gideon!" Mark grabbed her arm and raised it into the air like a heavyweight champion. When he let go, her arm fell to her side, more like a limp spaghetti noodle than a triumphant athlete.

In the end, the ice cream was worth it. The frosty strawberry flavor was perfectly sweet and refreshing in the heat of the evening. San Francisco was never this hot. Every day since she'd arrived a month ago had been scorching hot or filled with thunderstorms. Dani was finally getting used to the thick, moist air. Her hair, on the other hand, had been engaging in constant battle against the humidity. She was self-conscious about it at first, trying to tame the frizz she saw in the reflection of shop windows. Then Mark had told her the curls were cute. Since then, she'd let them be.

They ate their ice cream cones, and Mark walked her home from his parents' house. It was only a few blocks from Aunt Maggie's. Danielle let her hand dangle at her side and tried not to grin too broadly when Mark grabbed it casually. It was growing dark, and she spotted lightning bugs beginning to blink in the yards they passed. She was enjoying all the time they were spending together, but every time she thought he would kiss her - nothing happened. It was infuriating. After the comic convention. Under the stars around the campfire. Even sitting on Aunt Maggie's small loveseat. But no, Mark had continued to be a perfect gentleman, and it was driving her crazy.

At her front door, she gave him all the signals. She fidgeted with the bracelet on her wrist, turned her back to the door to face him. Danielle tried to channel her inner vixen and gave a breathy, "I had a great time tonight, Mark." It was exactly like the scene with Kevin James in Hitch. *Come on, Mark. Take the hint!* She pleaded with him in her head.

He licked his lips. "I-I did too. I think my family liked you."

"And what about you?" Danielle looked up at him.

His breath hitched in the quiet. "What?"

"Do you like me, Mark?" She blinked under her lashes, at the same time thinking herself ridiculous for trying tactics from the movies.

Maybe it was working though, because Mark softened. "How could I not, Danielle? You're perfect."

"Good." Since that was settled, she wrapped her arms around his neck and pulled him down. Just before their lips touched, she paused. "I like you, too."

At her words, he closed the distance between them and pressed his lips against hers. The cool sweetness of strawberry ice cream warred with the humidity and warmth of the evening and the undeniable heat between them. It had been a month of not-so-casual glances and stolen touches. Hours in the car and hours under the stars. To Dani, every single moment was leading up to this. She'd had kisses before, but none that grounded her so completely. She could grow roots and stand on that crooked front porch forever as the world went on around them. Her hands slipped up and tangled themselves in his thick hair and she leaned into his solid frame, desperate to get even closer.

*****

Mark enjoyed movies and comic books and video games. He adored teaching and he loved being a leader for the junior high youth group boys. But as much as Mark relished his various hobbies and interests, he had never found anything he liked doing as much as he enjoyed kissing Danielle Washington. To be fair, he hadn't kissed a girl since freshman year of college; so, it had been awhile. But dang, if this wasn't the most perfect kiss in the entire world.

Mark rested his hands on her waist. Usually he was on the smaller side, surrounded by his bigger, faster, stronger brothers and friends. But with Danielle tucked against him? He was ten feet tall. He wasn't planning to kiss her tonight. The secret of the investigation was still hanging over him, casting a shadow on even the most perfect evening. But when she pulled him close and admitted her feelings for him; he couldn't help it.

He savored the moment and ignored the nagging inside. But he pulled away, ending the kiss. He watched as she slowly opened her eyes, hazy below hooded lids.

"You are so beautiful." His words were ragged, barely a whisper heard above the sound of crickets and cicadas.

Danielle smiled lazily and reached up to kiss his cheek before turning to open the door. His hands fell away as she created distance between them.

"Goodnight, Danielle." Mark strolled back to his own house, hands in pockets and a grin he couldn't seem to shake. The coming weekend was Independence Day and Mark couldn't wait to have

Danielle by his side at the Flynn's celebration. Everyone would be there. Mandy's doctor was back and word around town was they were getting married. For years, their little circle of friends had been filled with singles. Especially since Rachel died, it had been Luke, Chrissy, Todd, Mark and Mandy. Sometimes a few of the Bloom sisters were around, and sometimes his brothers came in and out for various events. But there was a distinct lack of couples. In the last year, they had all gotten engaged or married. Except him.

Was he pushing this on Danielle because he didn't want to be the only bachelor? Mark considered what he had prayed for since college - the woman he would marry. He had prayed for someone pursuing God themselves. *Check.* Someone kind and generous; a hard-worker. *Check, check, check.* Then the things on the list his friends made fun of: someone who accepted him and enjoyed comics and games. *Double-check.* Someone beautiful? *Check yeah!* The pun made him laugh at his own cleverness.

Yep, it was official. Mark had fallen hard for the lovely baker from California. If it wasn't for the looming specter of the accusations and allegations, he would be moving much faster. He needed to tell her soon. The only thing that held him back was the possibility that she wouldn't believe him. What would he see in her eyes when he told her what he'd been accused of? It certainly wouldn't be the dreamy look of desire he'd seen tonight after the amazing kiss they'd shared. That was a look he could get used to.

Chapter 13

The Fourth of July was different here, Danielle mused. She barely noticed when the first patriotic flags went up on Main Street, but now the entire town was star-spangle bannered. Sure, people in San Francisco celebrated, and there were some professional fireworks shows. But it was nothing like this. American flags hung from every street light, and every shop window was decorated - hers included.

Everyone hired the same person; a local artist name Laura. She decorated everyone's windows with fireworks and flags. Bulldog's Bar and Grill even had a Statue of Liberty on their window. There was a tent selling fireworks at the QuikStop. Out of curiosity, Danielle stopped by. Astonished to see the sheer size of the fireworks for sale, she questioned Mark.

"Is it safe for people to have access to all these fireworks?"

Mark shrugged. "Sure, why not? I mean, yeah, there are some people who get hurt every year, but mostly it is fine. Man, my brothers and I used to spend all our money on firecrackers during this time of year. Roman candles, bottle rockets, M-80s." His voice was laced with nostalgia and he tipped his head to the left as he remembered.

"Wow. I never really thought about it. In California, the fireworks you can buy are pretty tame. Anything that can blow up is only for professionals."

"Seriously? That's so strange. We used to shoot roman candles at each other." Danielle's mouth fell open and she gasped. Mark raised his eyebrows. "You know, looking back, maybe there should have been a bit more oversight." He laughed and she couldn't help but smile.

"I can't imagine the trouble you five boys got in with free access to small explosives."

He chuckled. "Yeah. We used to ride our bike to the firework stand, spend all the money we had and carried our goodies back in plastic bags hanging from our handlebars. I remember Daniel, one time, bought the biggest brick of M-80s they had." Mark shook his head with a crooked smile. "Must have been a thousand in there. We sat on the river bank and tried to light them and throw them into the river just in time for them to explode as they hit the water. Got pretty good at it, too."

Danielle stared at him with her mouth wide. "Oh, my word. You could have blown off your hand!"

"Nah." Mark drew out the word. Then he tipped his head slightly for a moment. "Well, probably, yeah. There were a couple that blew up pretty close to us in the air. Probably why I can't hear anything."

"What do you mean?"

"What?!" Mark cupped his hand to his ear and spoke loudly.

Realizing that he was just joking, she leaned into him, nudging his shoulder with hers. They were sitting on the porch swing at Aunt Maggie's house, listening to and watching the fireworks explode around them. It was Friday night, and the fourth was tomorrow. Chrissy and Todd were hosting the big get-together at their house in the country. When Chrissy told Danielle that it was a 'pitch-in', Danielle's lost look must have given away her confusion.

"You know, everyone brings a dish to share, and then there is plenty of food for everyone." Chrissy gave the explanation while refilling salt and pepper shakers. Danielle had stopped by to give Chrissy the crocheted hamburger and french fries she made for the bistro.

With a dawn of understanding, Dani said, "Oh, you mean a potluck?"

"Is that what you call it? Round here, it's a pitch-in. 'Cause everybody pitches in."

Danielle had to admit, it made sense. But it would always be a potluck in her mind. Too many church gatherings lived in her memories where her mom carried in a hot baking dish of tater tot casserole or macaroni and cheese. She remembered making her way through the line, excited to see bags of chips or a bucket of fried chicken. As a child, she was always more excited about those than all the home-cooked options.

When the bakery closed on Friday, she took the remaining cookies and cupcakes, knowing they wouldn't open again until Monday. The desserts would be the perfect addition to the pitch-in. She couldn't help but give the phrase finger quotes in her mind.

It would be easy to get used to this. Small town life was quiet. Slower. She found herself sinking into the warm, sticky summer moments. Sweet and thick like good cookie dough; minutes lingered. Even when she was busy at the bakery, there was an unmistakable difference between working here and working at the bakery for Casey. The other day, someone picked up a cake they had ordered at the last minute. When Danielle told them the price was

$25; they wrote the check for $35, because they knew "it was an inconvenience, and" they "should have called sooner."

It left Danielle reeling and unsure how to respond. Aunt Maggie spoke up from her corner where she'd taken up residence every day and just said, "That's real kind of you, Lois. You give that grandson of yours a big birthday hug for me, okay?"

She'd been here a month. In some ways, it felt like she'd only just arrived. In others, like how close she felt to Mark, it felt like she'd been here for years. Now, when she walked down Main Street, she didn't see only strangers. Sure, she still stood out. But the looks were curious, not rude. Word had spread about her work at the bakery and she was becoming known for her own delicacies. She'd introduced a few new cupcake flavors with rave results.

Even Maggie admitted that it was nice to have some fresh life breathed into the bakery. They had plans to start offering donuts on Tuesdays and bagels on Fridays, to increase the morning traffic. It was Maggie's idea to let everyone know by providing donuts for the churches on Sunday morning.

The more she worked alongside her Aunt, the easier it was to move beyond what happened twenty-two years ago. Forgiveness hadn't happened overnight, but the resentment she was harboring faded with every shared recipe and each childhood memory Maggie shared.

Remembering the absolute chaos of the life she left behind in California, she just laughed and thanked God for his very clear direction. If she'd still had a job at Casey's, she didn't think she would have come. There was too much unknown out here. An unknown family. An unknown history of why her mother left. An unknown culture, typically portrayed as backwards and stuck in the past.

God had brought her here. And every evening spent watching the stars or playing video games with Mark made her want to stay even more.

She checked her phone, and a saw a text from Casey.

CE: Are you alive? Did you get run over by a tractor?

DW: Haha, very funny. I'm actually great. How are you?

CE: Oh, not too bad. You'll guess what happened with Adele though.

DW: What?!

CE: Can you talk?
It's knit night!

Danielle called her friend using the video chat app. When Casey answered and all the girls from Knit Night gathered around the phone to see her, she started to tear up.

"Oh, my goodness, guys. I miss you so much!"

"We miss you!" they chorused.

"Yeah, when are you coming back?" Liz spoke up from the back row.

"I don't know yet. My aunt is doing better, but she still has to take it easy. Plus, I basically run my own bakery here."

"Wow, that's really awesome." Casey's eyes were bright and Danielle was pleased there was no hint of jealousy.

"Adele, tell me what happened!" If there was news, Danielle wanted to hear it.

Adele covered her face with her hands, and Casey handed her the phone. When Adele had it, she held one of her hands in front of the camera, showing off a huge diamond ring on her left ring finger. "I'm engaged!" Adele practically shrieked in her excitement.

"What? Are you serious? How? You weren't even dating someone, right?" Danielle took on a serious tone. "You guys, exactly how long have I been gone? It's only been a month, right? Is Indiana some sort of time warp wormhole?" Her friends laughed at her attempt at humor.

"It's only been a month, I know. But Calvin had this-"

Danielle registered the name and interrupted. "Wait, wait! Calvin? As in, *your boss*, Calvin?"

Adele nodded, eager to continue. "Yes, we had this company to buy and it turns out Calvin doesn't like chocolate. So, we were spending all this time together and he admitted that he had feelings for me and well, next thing you know, we're engaged."

"Whoa, whoa. Slow down, chica. You are marrying someone who doesn't like chocolate?"

Everyone groaned. Clearly, they'd been over this point a couple hundred times. Adele rolled her eyes, "It's a long story. But, can you believe it?"

Danielle shook her head, "It's incredible, Adele. I'm so happy for you! He's a good man, right?"

"The best." Adele nodded firmly.

"Well, then. Yay!! When is the wedding?"

"It's in a month. Please say you can come?" Adele gave her an exaggerated begging face.

Danielle tried to hide her surprise. *A month?* "Oh, wow. Of course. I'll do everything I can."

Adele and her other friends in California squealed their excitement. *Sometimes there was too much estrogen at Knit Night*, she thought. "It'll be awesome to see you again!"

"Can't wait! How is everyone else doing?"

Danielle looked at the faces of her friends. All so different from each other, but connected by their love of God and beautiful yarn.

"All good here. How is Kentucky?" Emily asked.

"It's Indiana," Dani corrected, "but it's really good. I met a guy," she added sheepishly.

"What?!" she heard multiple voices and the video went jerky as multiple hands grabbed for control.

"Bring him to the wedding!" Liz had won the struggle, unsurprising with her nearly six-foot frame. She appeared on the screen; her red hair tied in a green scarf.

The sight of her engineer friend reminded her of the connection. "Oh, my goodness, Liz - guess what? You know Malachi?"

"You mean Malachi Dawson? My boss? The incredibly brilliant and equally irritating millionaire?"

Danielle nodded. "Yep. That's the one. Turns out he grew up here in the small town I'm in. And I'm dating his brother."

"Wow. Seriously? Small world. I honestly had no idea he was from Indiana."

"Apparently so. Do you know him well?"

"You could say that. He is pretty...intense. He gets distracted by his own thoughts a lot."

Danielle heard Aunt Maggie calling from the

other room. "Sorry, girls. I have to go, but I'm so glad we got to catch up. I miss you all!"

"We miss you more!"

"See you in a month."

Danielle saw Adele appear on the screen. "I'll send you the details! And don't worry about travel. I'll see if Calvin can cover it."

Danielle was both embarrassed and grateful for the offer. She'd been here for a month, but realized that she still didn't have any money. Was she really any better off than she'd been in California?

"Thanks, Adele. Bye now!"

"Bye!" A group shot of them all waving, and Casey blowing kisses was on the screen for a moment before the call ended and the screen went dark. She felt the silence of their absence acutely. Would she ever have that circle of friends here?

Chapter 14

When they arrived at the Flynn's house, Mark watched Danielle take it all in. There were more than thirty people at the party. Some sitting in camp chairs, others playing horseshoes and cornhole. Country music played from a surprisingly powerful Bluetooth speaker on the picnic table. There were kids running around, too. The sprinkler doused them as they ran through in swimsuits as parents looked on with amusement. Mark recognized Jessica Pruitt, the youth director from the church and her three kids. Mandy had a young girl clinging to her leg. Mark figured the doctor he'd heard so much about must be the one standing next to them.

Danielle's eyes were wide. She froze, cookies and cupcakes held close to her small frame. Mark wrapped an arm around Dani's waist and pulled her temple to his lips. "They're going to love you." Dani gave him a grateful smile, and he led her to the food table, where she placed her desserts next to a tray of brownies and an angel food cake with strawberries and whipped cream.

They turned back toward the excitement. Chrissy and Todd were on the far side, on opposite sides of a cornhole set, beanbags flying as they and two of the Bloom sisters shouted good-natured trash talk. Mark spotted Luke and Charlotte in a pair of camp chairs. Realizing he'd left his in the car, he pointed them out to Danielle and told her he would meet her there.

After retrieving the chairs from the trunk, he found Danielle and Charlotte deep in conversation, setting a date for drinks the following week. Mark set up the chairs and gestured for Danielle to sit. She seemed comfortable with Luke and Charlotte, at least. Neither of the Brands were originally from Minden, so there was a connection there. Minden didn't get too many people moving in. Although, now that Mark considered it, between Charlotte and Luke, Danielle and Mandy's doctor, Minden was becoming a popular destination. He asked Danielle what she'd like to drink and went to track down something cold for both of them.

On his way back with drinks, he detoured to see Mandy. "Hey, Mandy, how are you? Isn't it time I met the famous Doctor Pike?" He and Mandy had been friends for years, growing up in youth group and only a few years apart in school.

Mandy blushed and nodded. "Mark, this is my f-fiancé," she stumbled over the word, "Garrett Pike. Garrett, this is Mark. He's a good friend."

"Nice to meet you, Doctor." Mark tucked one drink under his arm and wiped the condensation from his hand before extending it to the tall, thin man.

Garret smiled and shook it. "Just call me Garrett, please."

"Garrett, then. When did you get back?"

Mandy looked at him with wide eyes. "Ma-ark!"

"What? He left, didn't he?" Mark recognized he was being impolite, but he needed to see for himself if the infamous Dr. Pike was the real deal.

Garrett turned to Mandy. "He's right, Amanda." Then, he turned back to Mark with a grim smile. "I've been back about three weeks. It was a mistake to leave. One I'll never make again." Garrett pulled Mandy to his side, kissed her temple, and she beamed.

Pleased to see his friend happy, he nodded. "Well, good. I'm glad you realize what a treasure this one is," he gestured to Mandy. "And who is this lovely lady?" Mark squatted to eye-level of the dark-haired little girl clinging to Mandy's leg.

Garrett responded, "This is Adelaide."

"Well, hello, Miss Adelaide." Mark reached a free hand out to shake hers solemnly. Then he gave her a goofy look, sticking out his tongue and closing one eye. She giggled.

"Miss Mandy is going to marry Unca Garrett!"

Mark chuckled. "I heard that. Is that okay with you?" Adelaide nodded, serious again. "I get to wear a pretty dress."

Mark let his eyes grow wide in exaggerated surprise. "Wow! That sounds super special. I can't wait to see it." The little girl's wide smile revealed two missing top teeth. He stood up with a smile on his face. There was something so fun about kids.

"Did I see you come in with someone?" Mandy asked.

The heat rose in his cheeks. "Yes. That's Danielle. She's Margaret Woodsen's niece. Be sure to come over and meet her sometime."

Mark made his way back to Danielle and the Brands, winding through clusters of conversation and not even attempting to dodge the sprinkler, enjoying the cool splatter of the water across his arms in the heat. He accidentally bumped into Chad Hall. Mark worked with Chad at Luke's, but never liked the guy. He had an opinion on everything and thought everyone needed to hear it. At Chad's confrontational "watch it!", Mark simply smiled and ducked away.

Before Mark sat down, he handed Danielle her

drink. Charlotte turned to him and asked about Gideon's job search. There was something cathartic about spending in the afternoon and evening with his friends. They played cornhole, the beanbag toss game. Danielle and Charlotte made relentless fun of the name while he and Luke handed them an embarrassing loss. Then Danielle hit a lucky streak and gave Todd his only loss of the day. Dinner was pulled pork, provided by Todd and Chrissy, and the dozens of side dishes and desserts everyone else contributed. After they went through the line, Mark noticed Danielle's plate was mostly empty. When he asked if she wasn't hungry, she pointed out nearly every dish had meat in it. Even the lettuce salad had bacon bits mixed in, and the cheesy potatoes had chunks of ham. Mark felt a twinge of guilt when he saw her plate of fruit salad and chips, when he piled his own with six different dishes. He'd be back for seconds, too.

"It's not a big deal, Mark. I'm used to it." Dani's words said it was fine, but her tone was sharp. Mark racked his brain for a solution. He spotted Chrissy and set his plate on his chair before heading her way.

*****

Stupid, hot, Indiana. Why does everything have bacon in it? Even the broccoli salad she'd been excited to see. *Nope. Bacon. Surrounded by food and she has fruit and chips. And dessert. At least there's dessert*, she comforted herself. Mark had just run off to who-knows-where, leaving her once again a third wheel alongside Charlotte and Luke.

When Mark returned, he brought Chrissy with him. "How y'all doing? I'm so glad you came!" Chrissy bounced with every step. "Oh, Dani! I totally forgot to tell you; Luke's got a veggie burger for you on the grill, it'll just be a minute!"

"Oh, wow. He doesn't have to-"

"Nonsense. I remembered you were vegetarian and wanted to make sure you had something! We put bacon in everything around here, you know?" Danielle coughed in surprise. Was Chrissy telepathic? "It was no big thing to grab a couple from the Bistro."

"Well, thank you. That was really thoughtful." Truthfully, Danielle was touched. She'd been sitting here complaining and bitter about the food, instead of grateful for being included and for the friends she'd made.

Yeah, okay, God. I got it.

Danielle ate the veggie burger, surprised at her own hunger. When she licked the mustard from her finger, she caught Mark laughing at her out the corner of her eye.

"What?"

"You're cute." His dark eyes twinkled, and the

corners wrinkled with his smile.

She rolled her eyes and grabbed a napkin to get the rest of the mess from her hands. "You're a dork."

"You like it." Mark winked.

Dani laughed. "Yeah, I guess I do." She leaned over and kissed him.

"Well, well, well. Markie Dawson. Didn't your momma teach you better than to associate with someone like her?" At the booming voice, Danielle turned her head from Mark and found a large, sweaty man in an American flag t-shirt with the sleeves cut off. His baseball hat was on backwards and he had a beer can in both hands. He tipped one up, finishing the last bit before tossing it into the trash can behind Danielle and Mark's chairs. A few drops of beer fell from the can as it arced over her head and land on her bare shoulders. *Gross.*

"Chad!" Luke barked.

"What? This is America, isn't it? I got a right to free speech." Chad popped the top on another beer and took a deep drink. "Besides, he's the one who brought *her* to the party." He slurred his words and sneered as he referred to Danielle. She froze in fear and disbelief.

Mark jumped to his feet and Danielle's eyes widened. *Oh no.* "Look, Chad. I'm not sure what your problem is, but you better knock it off."

Luke was up, too, and Todd stepped in from

behind. Todd grabbed the beer out of Chad's hand. "You've had enough, I'd say."

Chad looked around, and noticed the eyes on him. "How can you be okay with this? She doesn't belong here. And she doesn't belong with him!"

"Time to go, Chad." Luke and Todd both grabbed a shoulder and escorted Chad away. Todd returned before long and whispered to Charlotte before turning to the group that had gathered. "Okay, everybody! Make sure you get everything you want to eat. We're gonna pack up dinner before the flies eat it all! We'll light fireworks in an hour and a half."

Danielle's heart sank. That was all? This guy made a huge scene, and we were just going to ignore it? Wow.

Mark stood up and waved a hand. "Hey y'all. I wanted to say... This is Danielle. Most of you have met her, but in case you haven't - she's Margaret Woodsen's niece. And she's my girlfriend. And-"

Todd nodded. "And if you've got a problem with that, then you are welcome to leave."

Danielle's head spun. Warmth flooded her chest, relief and gratefulness in equal measure. And pride. How proud she was to be here with Mark, seeing his character on display. Was he aware that standing up and acknowledging her was exactly what she needed? At Todd's words, several others had nodded and called out their agreement. She felt seen. And accepted. Despite the ugliness of a few moments before, Mark accepted for who she was, nerdy t-shirts and crazy hair and all.

The crowd began to chatter, once more breaking off into smaller groups. Danielle felt eyes on her; and fought the urge to shrink into her camp chair. Instead, she stood and came up beside Mark, wrapping her hands around his upper arm and pressing herself close.

"Thank you." Danielle felt the familiar sting of tears behind her eyes and closed them. She couldn't convey her emotions in those two words, but attempting any more would release the flood. Too many years of judgment and hurt had bubbled close to the surface during the exchange with Chad. Another person who knew nothing about her and yet, deemed her unworthy.

"I'm sorry that happened to you. Please don't let his attack spoil Minden for you. He's..." Mark searched for the right words. "He's a challenge for most of us." Dani could sense Mark wanting to say something more, harsh and ugly about the man. She shouldn't, but she wanted Mark to denounce him as an idiot. A scourge on the town. A waste of air. And even as she thought it, her heart pinged with conviction. Passages from the Sermon on the Mount flickered through her mind. "You know that his opinion doesn't matter, right?" Mark's question was soft, so only she could hear.

She sighed and leaned her head on his shoulder before tipping her head back to talk towards his ear. "Theoretically, yeah, I get that. But in practice? I know that his vocalized opinion is the secret thought in many minds." And the tears she'd been fighting spilled over.

He stepped away and bent down to look in her watery eyes. "You don't know that."

"But I do, Mark!" She rubbed her upper arms with her hands crossed over her chest. "Don't you get it? I'm different here. Heck, I'm different everywhere." She tried to keep her voice low, but failed. "I don't fit neatly in a box and people struggle with that. Look around, Mark!"

Mark glanced around and then laid his hand on her upper back to lead her away. They stood behind the tree now. "Dani, don't you see? I'm different here, too! I put gel in my hair and wear tailored shirts. I own more shoes than my mother and I read comic books and watch anime. You think Minden has a box for hipster nerd? They don't. But people in this town have my back, no matter what."

Danielle shook her head quickly, refuting his argument. "It's different. You grew up here."

"No, the only difference is they know me. And they are getting to know you!" Mark was pleading now, her hands grasped in his. "It's easy to believe that people can't see past the surface. But they can. You just have to give them a chance." She nodded, unable to say more, and he pulled her close; hugging her and kissing her hairline before setting his chin on her head. Slow strokes of his hands on her upper back calmed her hot, shuddering breaths. "You belong here, Dani. As much as anyone. I'm sorry anyone said otherwise."

It was almost dark now and though they discussed leaving, Mark convinced her they should stay. They grabbed a blanket from his car and found a place to sit and watch the fireworks. After laying out the blanket, Mark sat and held an arm open for her. The invitation was irresistible.

Danielle sat on the hard ground and leaned into Mark as he sat with his legs spread out before him, one knee up and his weight resting back on one hand. The other, he wrapped around her waist. Dani laid her arm on top of it, her hand resting on top of his; their fingers intertwined. As the first fireworks exploded, Mark bent down and feathered a kiss at the back of her neck. She wasn't sure if it was the fireworks or her heart thundering in her ears.

Chapter 15

The rest of the weekend, Mark's cool-headed response to Chad simmered. During church, it bubbled slowly. In the afternoon, as Mark explored the open universe of an online game, it ate at him. Lying in bed Sunday night, Mark seethed at the gall of his coworker to say such hurtful things. Mark went to work Monday morning, angrier than ever and looking for a fight. He'd tolerated Chad's over-the-top opinions on every divisive political issue under the sun, giving perfunctory answers and rolling his eyes when Chad turned his back. But Chad had insulted Danielle and made her feel unwelcome, and that was unacceptable. And Mark wanted something done.

At church yesterday, Luke had promised they would talk today. When Mark stormed into Luke's office, he stepped around the stacks of papers and came up beside Luke's desk, which faced away from the door. "Well?!"

Luke turned, revealing the phone he was holding up to his other ear. "Okay. Thank you. I'll let you know." He lowered the cell phone and ended the call. "Have a seat, Mark."

"I don't want to take a seat, Luke. I want to know what you are going to do with Chad."

"Mark, have a seat." Luke wasn't often serious these days. He was too in love to let things drag him down. But the tone of his voice this time told Mark it wasn't optional. He picked up a binder from the seat of a chair along the wall and sat in its place.

"Fine. I'm sitting. Now, what are you going to do?"

Luke rubbed a hand through his hair. "What do you want me to do?"

"Luke, he's a racist and a drunk. You've got to fire him!"

"I'm not going to fire him."

"Are you freaking kidding me?" Mark jumped out of the chair and began to pace.

"There are things you don't know. But trust me. Firing him is the last thing he needs."

"I won't work with him."

Luke nodded. "That's understandable. I'll put him on a different crew."

Mark shook his head, still unwilling to believe

his friend refused to send Chad out on his butt. He opened his mouth, but Luke interrupted. "Do you trust me, man?"

Mark stopped pacing and looked at his friend. He'd known Luke for almost ten years, since Rachel had brought him home to Minden like a lost puppy. His shoulders slumped. "Yeah, I do." The anger drained out of him, his desire for revenge cooled by the reassuring words of his friend.

"Thank you. He was out of line. Is Dani okay?"

"I think so. We talked after the incident, but I didn't see her yesterday. I just -" Mark sat back down, leaning his elbows on his knees. He looked up to see Luke watching him. "I really like her, you know? She could be the one. And if a stupid, ignorant fool like Chad messes that up for me..."

Luke grinned and clapped his hands together. "Oh boy. You've fallen hard, Mark."

"That's what I'm trying to tell you! She's important."

Luke's grin faded, and he leaned forward in the ancient office chair. "Does she know?"

Mark looked at his shoes, classic black Converse All Stars. He shook his head. "No." Telling Danielle had crossed his mind a hundred times. Every time they were together, but something held him back.

"You need to tell her."

"I can't. It's gotta be over soon. I'll tell her when

it's over. I'll tell everyone when it's over." He looked up at his friend, afraid of what he would see. Judgment, pity. But Luke's eyes were friendly and understanding. His own words to Dani echoed through his mind. *People in this town have my back, no matter what.* Did he believe that?

Luke nodded and stood up. Mark followed. "Okay. But don't say I didn't warn you. Now get to work."

Mark saluted. "Yes, sir, Mr. Boss, sir." He cracked up and walked out the door, hearing Luke's muttering about disrespect behind him.

*****

Danielle spent Sunday with Aunt Maggie at the bakery again. Together, they prepped for the bistro and stocked the display case. She tried not to focus on the events of the previous evening, but they continued to eat at her. There was no one to talk to, though. Aunt Maggie? Based on what happened years ago, it was just as likely she secretly agreed with Chad. Even if she didn't agree with him; could she really understand? Danielle didn't think so. Instead, she acted like nothing was wrong, even though the need to tell someone what happened tore at her.

That evening, Danielle was lying on the uncomfortable guestroom bed scrolling through posts on a popular online message board. Every new post reminded her she should go to sleep, but the endless stream of distraction dulled the melancholy ache in her chest. The text message alert popped up over a teaser from the newest Star Trek movie. It was Adele.

AW: I'm so excited to see you at the wedding. I'll send a formal invite if you give me your address, but the wedding is August 1st. It's in Napa at Copper Sunset Winery.

> **DW: Thanks for the info. How are the plans coming?**

AW: It's crazy trying to pull everything together so quickly! But I am beyond ready to be married.

Dani typed out a text message, then deleted it. The question would reveal to Adele how significant her feelings for Mark had become. She typed it again, and pressed 'Send'.

> **DW: How did you know**

Calvin was the one?

**AW: Wow! Getting deep,
    aren't we?**

She read the text message just as Adele's name and picture flashed on the screen as an incoming call.

"Girl," she greeted her friend, "you didn't need to call! I'm sure you have more important things to do."

"Nah, I'm done for the night. It's like nine o'clock. Past my bedtime."

"Well, it's eleven o'clock here, and I will be at the bakery at five to start baking."

"Oh, fudge. Should I let you go?"

"No, it's okay. I couldn't sleep anyway," Dani admitted to her friend.

"What's going on, Dani?"

Danielle sighed in the dark. "Something happened yesterday. This stupid, drunk guy made a big scene about me being in Minden and because Mark was with me." She covered her face with her hand, feeling the need to hide even though Adele couldn't see her.

"Well, that's crappy," Adele was straightforward, something Dani had loved about her ever since they met.

"Right? It's just throwing me. I thought I was making a home here."

"So what? Just because one guy doesn't see how awesome you are doesn't mean Indiana can't be home."

Adele's stance made sense, but Dani's confidence wavered. "But what if it's not just one guy? What if he's just the one brave enough to say it? I miss San Francisco. I miss living someplace where not every person has blond hair and blue eyes." *Okay, that's an exaggeration, but the sentiment is there.*

Adele was silent for a moment. "Other than this incident, do you like it there?"

"Well, yeah. I do." She thought of the good things about Minden. "It's been surprisingly easy to get to know people. And I've gotten to see how everyone has taken care of Aunt Maggie. All the little small-town things - it feels like Gilmore Girls, I'm telling you. There was a Fourth of July parade, and Adele, half the parade was just every single firetruck in the county." She laughed. "And the stars out here! It's unreal. It's like the middle of the dessert."

She could hear Adele's smile, "Sounds awesome, Dani."

She let the silence linger. "Yeah. It really is."

"You want to know what I think?"

"Yeah, you know I do."

"Well, good. Because I'm going to tell you."
Adele was honest, but kind. "If you stay, not every
person will be blue-eyed with blond hair. And that's
a pretty awesome impact."

Dani considered her friend's point. Could she be
the difference? How much impact could she really
have, though?

"I'll think about it."

"Okay." As though she could sense her friend's
need to reflect on the discussion, Adele changed the
subject. "I need your PayMe account email, and I'll
send you money for plane tickets for you and Mark.
I'm dying to meet him!"

Dani smiled. "I haven't even asked if he will
come with me, so hold your horses."

"Horses? Have you ridden a horse out there? Do
people, like, ride them around town and stuff?"

"Adele, this isn't Texas. No, I haven't ridden a
horse." Then she considered Poppy and Rose, who
she'd met at the party yesterday. Rose said they kept
horses at Bloom's farm. Maybe Mark would take
her riding sometime.

"Well, that's too bad. I've always wanted to ride
a horse," Adele said pensively.

"Well," Dani laughed, "I'm sure if you tell your
ridiculously rich fiancé about that little dream, he'd
buy you one."

Adele laughed and agreed. "You're probably
right, he would. Which is crazy, right? It feels like a

fairy tale." She added an exaggerated romantic sigh which turned to giggles.

Dani grinned. "I'm so happy for you, Adele."

"Thanks, Dani." Then, her voice serious, "Are you going to be okay?"

"Yeah, I'm good." She tipped her head back for a moment and closed her eyes. God had blessed her beyond measure with friends like Adele. "Thanks for talking though. I better get some sleep." She was already dreading the incessant screech of her Dr. Who alarm clock.

"Goodnight, Dani.

"Goodnight." The hum of the connection went silent and the cool, blue light from her phone illuminated the small room before disappearing, cloaking the room in darkness. She set her phone on the side table and settled into the feather pillow. With a contented smile, she drifted off to sleep.

Chapter 16

"Are you sure there isn't anything else you want to do while we are in California?" Mark readily agreed to go to the wedding with her, and they made plans to fly to San Francisco. Mark called Malachi and he invited them to stay at his condo for the trip. Mark seemed excited at the prospect of seeing his brother, and they booked tickets for a few extra days.

"I'm sure. All my friends will be at the wedding. Other than them, there is nothing waiting for me there."

The wedding was three weeks away. This weekend, Aunt Maggie insisted that she could handle the bakery counter on Saturday morning, and she waved Danielle off when Mark stopped by to see her. They walked hand-in-hand to Minden Park, just off Main Street, and wandered through the modest farmer's market. It was minuscule compared to the markets she frequented in California, although the prices were much lower. Mark bought a cup of coffee from Holly at the bistro's table and they strolled from table to table looking at crafts, homemade jellies and salsas, and produce. They stopped to talk to Poppy Bloom; her table mounding with ripe vegetables and berries in cute wicker baskets. Vibrant reds, greens, purples, and blues contrasted with the simple white tablecloth for an eye-catching display.

Mark greeted her first. "Hey, Poppy."

"Heya, Mark. Danielle, right?"

Danielle nodded with a smile. "Yep, good memory."

"How are things up at the farm? This all looks awesome," he gestured to the produce.

"Oh, pretty good. It's busy for us this time of year. Lily's got weddings every weekend, and I've got a dozen different plants to harvest. Daisy tries to help, between all her renovation projects on the house."

Danielle tried to keep track. Too many flowers. "Wait, how many sisters do you have?" Then, realizing how she must sound, "I'm sorry, I don't mean to be rude."

Poppy laughed. "No worries. It's a common question! There are six of us, plus my brother, Hawthorne."

"Whoa. And you're all named after..." Danielle trailed off, afraid to finish the question.

"Flowers?" Poppy grinned, "Yep. My parents love nature and well... here we are: Lily, Lavender, Daisy, Dandelion, Rose, and Hawthorne. And Poppy." She did a little curtsy.

Dani's mouth fell open. "Did you say *Dandelion*?"

"Hah, yeah. Poor Andi. She hates it when people call her by her full name. So, of course, we do it as often as possible," she said with a mischievous grin.

"How is Andi? Still in the Middle East?" Mark asked.

"Yeah, her third deployment. Afghanistan this time. She swears she's done after this though. We'll see." Poppy shrugged.

"We'll keep praying for her to come home safely." Mark's words were genuine and fervent and Dani felt a rush of affection. He spoke of his faith so openly. She found herself once again wishing she had that confidence.

"Thanks, Mark. Our family really appreciates that." Poppy deftly turned the topic to the produce, pointing out which crops were especially flavorful. They bought a basket of tomatoes and some sweet corn, after Danielle admitted she hadn't had any yet this summer. Danielle bought a bunch of blackberries and raspberries for the bakery, explaining to Mark they were for pies.

Mark looked at her. "You're going to make pie?"

She gave him a confused look. "What?"

"I *love* pie. Are you going to make blackberry pie?" He turned to face her, "This is a very serious question, Danielle Washington." He drew her close, "Don't toy with me."

She laughed and spun away. "I don't know..." She looked tipped her head in false indecision. Teasing him was endlessly entertaining. "I thought I might just make frosting with them."

"Don't make me beg." He grabbed her hand and got down on one knee.

Her heart stopped. Oh my, what an image! What was he doing? People were watching!

"Danielle Washington, will you do me the great honor" Mark's solemn face broke into a grin "of making me a pie?" The people around broke into amused laughter.

"Oh, you! Get up right now." At her exasperation, Mark laughed and stood up. "Yes, I'll make you a pie. What are you, twelve years old? So embarrassing!"

"She said yes, everybody!" he held her hand in the air and looked around the crowd with a beaming smile. The crowd applauded and Danielle ripped her hand from his to hide her face in her hands.

"Here's your bags, Danielle. Get him out of here, would ya?" Poppy held out the produce they had purchased and nodded to Mark with a grin. "You guys are good together." Danielle's smile grew, so wide now she felt like her cheeks would pop with the unfamiliar stretch.

"Thanks, Poppy. I think so, too," she admitted.

They continued walking through the market, collecting glances and smiles from people who'd seen Mark's ridiculous display. A teenager came running up to Mark, basketball shorts hanging way too low and tall white socks inside black slide sandals. "Hey! Mr. Dawson, what's up?"

Mark gave the man a complicated handshake. "Hey Troy! How's your summer been?"

"Good." The young man shrugged. "Football practice starts soon and all that."

"Oh? You playing this year?"

Troy gave in to the grin, forgetting to play it cool. "For sure, man! You gonna be at the high school retreat next weekend?"

"Yep, I'll be there," Mark affirmed.

"Awesome. I'm gonna crush you at Call of Duty."

Mark laughed. "You wish, dude."

Danielle watched the exchange with amusement. Someone called Troy's name and just like that, he was gone again.

"Pull up your shorts, Troy!" Mark called, and Troy waved an arm in the air in acknowledgment, yanking his shorts up on the opposite hip while picking his way through the small crowd.

Mark shook his head and turned back toward Danielle. "Kids."

"Former student?"

"Yep, and current youth group member."

"He's very..." she searched for the word, trying not to seem judgmental.

"Young?" Mark supplied with raised eyebrows.

"Exactly."

"The thing is, I met him four years ago. And he's completely different than he was as a sixth grader. But entirely the same, too. Does that make sense?"

She shook her head with a laugh. "Not even a little."

Mark chuckled. "Yeah, probably not. It's hard to explain. Like, I watch these kids grow up. But after they are in my class, I see them maybe once a week at most. They turn into adults when I'm not looking. But they are still babies."

"Must be even stranger when it is your own kids," she added.

"Probably. The changes are so gradual." Mark was looking into the distance, deep in thought.

"Then," she tried to lighten the mood, "one day

you look up and all five of your sons are adults and not one has the decency to bring home a girl and start having some grandkids." Mark threw his head back and laughed at the obvious reference to his mother.

"True, true. But Danielle, let me tell you something." Mark turned to her, stopping in the middle of the sidewalk, letting people navigate around them. He stepped close.

"What?" Dani's breath caught at his sudden closeness. She inhaled the aroma of his cologne.

He turned his head slightly to speak into her ear, the warmth of his breath tickled her neck. "If things continue like they are with us, you'll see me on one knee again. And I won't be asking for pie." Then Mark turned back and continued walking. Leaving her behind as though he hadn't just shaken her entire core. Dani blinked, breaking her stare from the place he'd been standing moments ago.

Mark grabbed her hand nonchalantly and pointed out a table ahead of them, completely ignoring the bombshell he'd just dropped.

Well, two can play that game. She struggled to find a safe topic among the whirlwind of thoughts in her head. "How old are your very first students now?"

"Oh man. Don't remind me! They graduated last year and most of them are in college."

"That must be kind of cool, though. Knowing

that you helped them get there."

"A few, yeah. I like to think I make a difference."

"I'm sure you do. I bet you are a great teacher."

Mark gave her a soft kiss. "Thanks, Danielle. I'm really glad you think so."

*****

When Danielle mentioned to him that she wanted to try horseback riding, Mark figured it was another opportunity to show her all the great things about living in the country. So, he texted Rose and she agreed to let them come up to Bloom's Farm and take out a couple trail horses. With Danielle in the passenger seat, Mark pulled into the gravel drive and drove under a rustic sign, declaring Bloom's Farm and Vineyard. He recalled that Poppy mentioned grapes she'd started growing last year. The white wooden fence led them up the driveway, and they passed the large event barn that sat on the front portion of the property.

They continued toward the main house, which Daisy was determined to turn into a bed and breakfast. From the look of it, there was still an awful lot of work to do. Mark turned left behind the house and drove them to the new barn down in the valley. Unlike the old, wooden barn that had been renovated for events, this barn was sided with metal and had partially open sides. Mark knew the farm had goats, pigs, chickens and horses. Danielle had only mentioned horseback riding, but he figured she needed the full experience. Bloom's Farm was a local landmark, providing tons of family fun with their pumpkin patch, event barn, and petting zoo days.

Rose came out to greet them, wiping her hands on her dusty jeans. "Hey Mark! Danielle, it's good to see you again."

"You too, Rose. Thanks so much for letting us come ride the horses." Mark was pleased to hear the genuine appreciation in Dani's voice. She seemed excited for their little adventure. "My city upbringing didn't exactly include a lot of exposure to farm animals."

"Well, you came to the right place. Let me show you around a little." She waved them inside the metal building, where they walked in an aisle between fenced-in areas. Mark could see how each area contained a different animal, and how the pens were open to areas outside the barn as well.

Rose stopped by the pen containing the goats and leaned on the fence, putting one boot up on the bottom fence rail. "These are my babies. My goats are the first animals I ever took care of on my own. We've got about thirty goats, and about ten kids already this season. I've got a couple more that are due any day now, too."

Mark watched Danielle as she observed the goats. She turned to him, "Look how little that one is!"

Rose smiled. "That's Roscoe. He's only about three days old, actually. His twin sister, Rachel is over there." She pointed to another small kid a few yards away.

After the goats, Rose took them to the horse stables, located at the farthest side of the barn. Three horses were already saddled and ready to go. Rose introduced them to Cappuccino and Espresso, the horses they would be riding. Her own horse was named Mocha. Rose gave them each an apple to feed to their horse, and showed them where a couple sugar cubes were stored in the saddle bag for treats during their ride. Danielle was absolutely enthralled with her horse and Mark watched as she went from a gentle touch on the horse's nose to long, firm rubs along Cappuccino's neck.

Mark gave Espresso the apple and a few friendly pats. He couldn't hear what Danielle was whispering to Cappuccino, but he suddenly found himself jealous of the animal as she played with her horse's mane and talked to her in a low voice.

Rose brought over a step stool and was patiently talking Danielle through the process of getting on the saddle. When he grabbed the saddle horn and attempted to place his foot in the stirrup, Mark realized his mistake: skinny jeans were *not* designed for horseback riding. At least not his one-hundred-dollar designer brand dark wash ones. He quickly stepped out of view and attempted to readjust. He was in the middle of a couple quick, deep squats, trying to stretch out the tight fabric of his jeans when he heard the snickers.

He froze mid-squat and looked up to see that his horse had shifted position just enough to leave his impromptu exercise routine in clear view of the girls. Danielle looked down from atop Cappuccino, and pressed her lips together in a hidden smile. "Doing okay down there?"

He stood up and cleared his throat. "Umm, yep. Just stretching a bit. Wouldn't want to get stiff or anything." He squirmed as they nodded behind poorly disguised laughter and he quickly moved to Espresso's side again. Though the material squeezed his thigh as he lifted his shoe to the stirrup, he ignored the constriction and pushed himself up and into the saddle. *It's been a long time since I did that,* he mused. But, as uncomfortable as he might be at the moment, he was on the horse. *Who needs blood flow to their legs anyway?* His ears were hot as he looked over to Danielle. He never claimed to be a cowboy, right?

Chapter 17

Horseback riding was a completely new experience for Danielle. Rose led the way, and their horses ambled after Mocha on the trails. Danielle didn't have to do much besides make sure she didn't fall off. At first, Cappuccino seemed alarmingly large, but when Danielle offered her an apple and looked at the strong creature closer, she saw an intelligence there. The light brown mare seemed excited to be out, occasionally nipping at the long grass brushing Danielle's legs as they rode past. But Cappuccino followed Mocha patiently.

The ride was a beautiful tour of Bloom's Farm. The unmarked path crossed pastures and wound through wooded areas along the creek. From atop a hill, Danielle could see the entrance and the event barn on one side, and the fields of produce and grapevines on the other. Everything was green and lush, and the sky opened in front of her. Somehow, the sky seemed bigger out here. In the midst of its size, she didn't feel as insignificant, either.

Rose was a great tour guide, telling them the history of the farm and her family. Apparently, Rose went to school to be a veterinary technician, but ended up coming back to the farm to help her father as he got older. There was a twinge in Danielle's heart, in the company of two people who still had their parents and were so close to them. Why didn't she get to have that? She lost her mom when she was twenty-five, her mom only sixty. It was a familiar argument; one she'd had with God a dozen times already this year. Tempted to slip into the melancholy, she resolved instead to focus on the things she did have and the family she had just discovered with Aunt Maggie. When the ride was over, Rose unsaddled the horses and handed them each a brush, leaving them alone to talk and groom the horses.

"What did you think of your first riding experience?" Mark asked.

Danielle ran the brush along Cappuccino's coat and patted her lovingly. "I think I'm going to be sore tomorrow," she said with a grimace, bending her knees up toward her waist. "But it was fun to see the countryside like that. The farm is beautiful."

Mark nodded. "You'll have to come back in the

fall. They have apple picking and a pumpkin patch. Hawthorne even gives hayrack rides. Have you ever been?" His words seemed innocuous enough, but she heard the unspoken question. Would she still be here in the fall? Dani shook her head lightly and then continued brushing the honey-colored horse, answering no to the obvious question and unable to answer the other.

*****

Aunt Maggie and Danielle kicked off their new morning menu on Tuesday with fresh donuts. Even Norm came over from the restaurant to have one, letting them know it was a great idea. Danielle was relieved to see no jealousy on his face as he licked the sticky glaze from his fingers. She poked her head out the door and was pleased to see despite the heavy traffic they'd had, the bistro seemed to be busy as well.

Since Mark had the high school retreat starting Wednesday, they went back to the creek and had another campfire. He would be gone through Sunday. The church took the kids to a camp in southern Indiana where they went hiking and swimming.

Their campfire had no hotdogs this time, and extra bug spray. Instead of chairs, they laid on a blanket and looked straight up at the sky. Only

Dani's head rested on his chest, their bodies perpendicular on the blanket. As tempted as she was to snuggle up next to him, she knew it was a bad idea. They were too alone out here.

They looked for satellites and talked. Conversations drifted effortlessly from topics of God to Gotham. She laughed until her ribcage ached and she thought she might have to sneak into the woods like a true country girl. She might be considering staying in Minden, but she drew the line there. *Peeing in the woods? I don't think so.*

Instead, she sat up and curled her arms around her knees; watching the fire instead of the stars. "Do you ever wish you could be someone else?" she asked him.

Mark sat up, too. "What do you mean?"

"Like, do you ever see a stranger on the street and think, 'I wonder what their life is like?'"

The fire snapped in the silence as she waited for Mark's answer. "I think for me, it wasn't strangers. I've wished to be my brothers, though."

"Really?" It surprised her. Mark seemed confident around his brothers. Unlike her, he seemed totally comfortable being himself.

"Yeah. I mean, with five of us, even with the best parents in the whole world, you're fighting for attention. Daniel always had it - football games and awards ceremonies. Malachi was the same way, except with Trivia Bowl and science fairs. I just always felt like I faded into the background. That's way I became the funny one, I guess. But it's exhausting to be the happy, funny one all the time." Mark paused, staring at the fire. "But if I'm not? I'm afraid they won't see me. Like I might disappear." He turned to look at her, as though afraid to see how she would react to his revelation.

She scooted closer to him. "Oh, Mark. Nothing could make you disappear. I hope you don't feel like you have to put on that front for me."

Mark's teeth flashed, and he shook his head. "No, I really don't. That's one of the things I love about you."

Her sharp intake of air was audible in the stillness.

"What I meant was-" Mark's words were cut off by her lips against his. She felt him jolt with surprise at the sudden impact of her shoulder against his.

The kiss was over as quickly as it started. "Don't take it back," she whispered, still leaning into him. Her eyes stayed glued shut as she lingered in the closeness. Dani couldn't bear it if he didn't mean it. Every moment spent with the man next to her had shown him to be sweet and caring and generous. He was her best friend. Mark seemed to understand her in a way few people ever had. And heaven help her, she loved him. She opened her eyes to find his.

"Never," he agreed. Then, Mark touched his lips

gently to hers again. "I love you, Danielle."

The tingle from his lips ran down her spine and Danielle's entire body hummed with pleasure. "I love you, too."

*****

Danielle kissed him again and his heart raced. It was the perfect evening. Stars, campfire, discussions of Batman and Dragon ball Z. And the love of a beautiful woman. Did it get any better? Again, his conscience prickled. He loved her. And she loved him. She'd just admitted it. He should tell her about the investigation. He'd almost told her at the farmer's market, but he convinced himself there were too many people around and someone might hear.

Mark couldn't use that excuse here. It was just the two of them for miles. And yet, he knew if he said something, it would ruin the moment. Instead of being the night they had professed their love for each other, it would forever be the night he told her he'd been accused of abusing a student.

Nope. He couldn't drop that bombshell on her and then leave for five days. What kind of boyfriend would that make him? *I'll tell her when I get back.* How much longer could the investigation drag on, anyway? How hard was it to prove he was innocent? It would be a lot easier to answer that question if he actually knew the details of the accusation. That had to be the most frustrating part. He didn't know who or what or when. But especially, he still couldn't figure out why. That question had circled around in his head for hours as he drove the lawn mowers each day.

Why would someone say this? Why would they lie? If he was found innocent, would he even get to know the details then? Or would it still be an unknown, hanging over his head? For now, he reminded himself to be patient. He could tell Danielle on Sunday, and then maybe he could go to Steve and get an update about the investigation. His friend and boss owed him that much, right? For now, he was just going to soak in the moment.

Three nights later, as he sat in the back of campfire service on Friday evening, students he recognized knelt before the cross during the final worship song. Southern Indiana was its own kind of beautiful. There were tons of hills and trees, and creeks and trails wound through the forest. There was blessedly little cell phone reception, really giving the students a chance to connect with each other and with God.

He'd made his own decision for Christ at a similar retreat in high school. With the guitar penetrating the night and students kneeling in front of the cross, he was flooded with memories of his own commitment to live each day for his Father. It had been twelve years since he was that awkward teenage boy. Now he figured he was a mostly unawkward adult. And he knew less now than he thought he knew back then.

On the walk back from the campfire site, he felt his phone vibrating. Surprised, since they hadn't had signal all day, he pulled it out to see dozens of unread text messages. Then, Steve's name flashed on the screen. Eagerness to hear the news that the investigation was over had him fumbling for the green button as he stepped off the narrow trail and let others pass.

"Yes, this is Mark."

His friend's deep voice crackled in his ear. "Mark, it's Steve Morton. I've been trying to get ahold of you. Is everything okay?"

Mark's heart raced. *Tell me it's over!* "What? Yeah, I'm just down south a ways and don't have good reception."

"Oh. Well, in that case, you haven't heard. I have some bad news."

Chapter 18

Mark sagged against the tree as campers continued to hike, unknowing, past him. They laughed and sang, oblivious to the fact his entire world just collapsed in a giant, steaming pile of ashes. Someone leaked the investigation to the local media. The news station in Terre Haute picked it up, and it was all over social media and the radio. Tomorrow, it would be on the evening news. His name and picture, along with a heavily bolded headline proclaiming the allegations, splashed on air for everyone to see. Already, Steve said he'd been getting dozens of phone calls from media and parents.

It was eleven o'clock at night, the news first surfaced around six. Mark wondered briefly if

Danielle heard. Then his parents. He slid down the tree, the rough bark grabbing his shirt and scraping his back, but he barely felt it. The moist ground welcomed him, and he laid his head on his knees, finally letting the tears overtake him. Far enough off the trail that darkness cloaked his hiding place, the last few campers passed unaware. He'd go see Jessica when he finally got up. There was no choice but to leave camp immediately and drive home; despite the late hour.

But for the moment, Mark just wanted to disappear into the crevice of the hundred-year old oak. He leaned his head back against the tree, wishing it would slowly open up and swallow him, like the ancient character of a video game. The same unanswered questions raced through his mind. Why was this happening? Who would say such a thing about him? Steve told him a few details, since it was now public knowledge. Three girls claimed he had rubbed their shoulders and made inappropriate comments toward them. The reality hit him like a punch in the gut. Three? Why had three girls made accusations against him that were entirely false? It still had his head spinning. Would his word stand up against three separate accusers? Who would believe him when the story sounded so damning?

Would Danielle believe him? Would his friends? Even Luke, whom he'd told about the investigation, would have to question the validity of his denial in the face of three stories. Nothing like this had happened in Minden as long as he could remember. The occasional drug charge or bar fight caught the local's attention and was gossiped about over coffee. But nothing so serious as this. The gossip-mongers in Minden would be talking about this for months. Probably even after the investigation.

God, why would you let this happen? It was bad enough when it was private and I worried about the outcome, but now everyone knows. Everyone thinks I'm a predator. I've always tried to live for you and serve you, and now all my work is tainted. What am I supposed to do if I can't be a teacher? If I have to leave Minden? They are lying, Father! Please, please, don't let them ruin me with their lies.

Even in the still and quiet night, Mark heard no answer. He waited for what seemed like hours. The tears were dried now; his head aching in the aftermath. Mark stood slowly and prayed for strength for the days to come. He suspected his prayer would be repeated daily, maybe hourly.

Jessica looked at him with sympathy after he knocked on her cabin door. The look in her eyes told him she'd heard the news. "Come on in, Mark." She had a private cabin, as the director in charge of camp this week. He followed wordlessly. "Are you okay?"

He barked a bitter laugh. "No. Should I be?"

The corner of her lips turned down. "No, I suppose not."

He sighed. "I'm sorry I didn't tell you. I should have. I kept thinking it would go away. That I would be found innocent and then it would disappear, like it never happened."

"You should have told me," she agreed. "But, Mark, I've served with you for five years. I've never seen even a hint of impropriety. You have a calling to work with these kids. And when this is all over, I want you right back at youth group on Wednesday nights. Okay?" He nodded, the lump in his throat making it impossible to speak. She patted his arm. "I wish I didn't have to, but you have to leave camp tonight."

He cleared his throat. "Yeah. I figured."

"It's going to be okay, Mark. Alright?"

"Sure." His lack of faith was obvious and Jessica raised an eyebrow.

"Would you let me pray for you?" He agreed and Jessica grabbed her Bible from the bedside table. She prayed Psalm 5 over him, her confident voice declaring David's prayer of refuge. Mark let the words wash over him, amazed at the relevance of a prayer from thousands of years before. He smiled and more tears escaped, this time of thankfulness. This was what was missing. He should have told his friends and family when the accusations were first brought. The situation could have been surrounded with prayers for justice and truth to prevail, instead of enveloped in secrecy and shame. Jessica wrapped up her prayer and Mark gave her a hug.

"Thanks, Jess. Keep praying for me, okay? I'm going to need it."

He grabbed his things from the cabin and told the high school boys he'd see them next week. Above all else, he didn't want to distract them from whatever God was doing in their life this weekend. They weren't allowed to have cellphones, so they shouldn't find out about anything until they got back home.

It was almost one in the morning now, and Mark was exhausted. The day was filled with swimming and hiking, and he was tired even before the emotional roller coaster he'd been on since Steve's call. He pulled into a hotel about forty-five minutes away from camp and grabbed a room. When he woke up, he'd have to face the problem head on, but for now, he prayed for restful sleep.

Mark didn't wake until after nine the next morning and said a quick prayer of thanks for the crisp white sheets and soft bed that cradled him all night. Sleep had been blessedly deep, overtaking him in minutes after crawling under the fluffy comforter. He picked up his phone and looked at it hesitantly, even closing one eye and holding it at a distance. Twenty-five missed calls. Forty-two text messages. Mark scanned the list of calls, unsurprised to see his mother's name listed several times, along with Luke and Chrissy and Mandy. Nothing from Danielle. Mark flipped to the text messages, reading messages of support from several friends, and cringing at the messages of hate from numbers he didn't recognize and from some he did. Nothing from Danielle since yesterday. *She despises me.*

He called his mom and closed his eyes at her familiar voice through the phone. "Marco? Are you okay?"

"I'm okay, Mom."

"Where are you?" His mother's voice held trepidation and worry.

"I'm at a hotel near Bloomington. I needed to leave camp last night after the news broke, but I couldn't make it home."

"Oh, son. I'm so sorry. Why didn't you tell us?"

"I'm sorry, Mom. I should have said something when I found out, but I was so ashamed. I didn't want you to think any less of me. It's not true, Mom. You have to believe me." The idea his mother could believe the lies about him was painful.

Donna scoffed. "Of course, *cuore mio.* I never doubted you. All these busybodies outside your house have no idea what they are talking about."

Mark straightened. "Outside my house? What

do you mean?"

"Oh, the news van is there. Don't go to your house, sweetheart. You come here, okay? I'm making raviolo." Oh boy. His mother only made raviolo when she was upset. The lengthy process gave her something to do with her hands. Oh, this was bad.

"Thanks for the heads up, Mom. I'm still about three hours out." He tripped over the next question. "Have... have you seen Danielle at all?"

"No, sorry dear." After a pause, her voice was higher, filled with false cheer. "I'm sure she's at the bakery, though. Do you want me to call Margaret?"

"No, no. I'll talk to her when I get back."

"Okay dear. Drive carefully. I love you."

"I love you, too, Mom." Mark felt the familiar thickness in his throat. The presence of more tears seemed impossible and he blinked them away.

"It's going to be okay, *Marco*."

"Keep praying, Mom."

"Of course, *cuore mio*. I couldn't stop if I wanted to."

Chapter 19

Saturday morning, Danielle took a break from the bakery and popped over to the bistro. After yesterday's success with serving bagels in the morning, she was grateful for the slower pace of Saturday. There wasn't much baking to do, since they closed Sundays. She was dying for a latte and walked up to the counter. After a moment, she became aware that the conversation in the bistro had slowly fizzled as she stood there.

"Morning, Dani. What can I get you?" Chrissy was subdued. Her normal, cheerful smile was conspicuously absent as she made broken eye contact with Danielle.

"Ummm," Danielle looked around, seeing a dozen eyes on her from across the room. "I'll take an iced chai latte?"

"Coming right up." Chrissy turned to make her latte.

Still nothing but whispers. Danielle tried not to listen.

"I think she was dating him, right?"

"How could she be with someone like that?"

Was she hearing this correctly? Or filling in blanks with her mind that weren't there?

"Chrissy?" she called. When Chrissy was close, she asked "What's going on?"

Chrissy waved her hand. "There's a dumb rumor going around. Don't worry about it."

Dani frowned. "What is it?"

"It's about Mark." She exhaled. "People are saying he is under investigation by the school board."

"For what?"

"It's not true." Her tone was sharp, leaving no room for arguments.

Dani straightened. "Chrissy, tell me. Or I'll find someone who will."

"There are some female students saying he touched them inappropriately." Chrissy slumped, defeated by the serious admission.

Danielle blinked. What? That couldn't be possible. But why would they say it if it wasn't true. "How many?" she asked blankly.

"What?"

Danielle's voice was hard. "How many students are saying that he... *touched* them?"

"I heard there were three involved in the investigation," Chrissy admitted.

"And you don't believe them?" She remembered telling the general manager at the hotel where she worked about the supervisor getting handsy in the back office. Being told *He's a good man, why would he do that? He's worked here for ten years. You aren't doing yourself any favors by fabricating stories.* It had been her word against his. And hers was dismissed. The memory of how powerless she felt would haunt her. She would never rob another victim of that power by doubting their story.

Chrissy shook her head. "I know Mark. I've known him my whole life. I won't believe he would do something like that."

Dani felt the heat in her face. "But isn't that what people say all the time? Like, they lived next door to a serial killer for ten years but he was the nicest guy and watered their plants while they were on vacation?"

"I guess." Chrissy chewed her lip. "But it's Mark! He is one of the nicest guys I've ever met. Look, he's got to be absolutely devastated this is happening. At least wait until they close the investigation before you bail on him, okay?" Chrissy's blue eyes pleaded with Danielle. "He really cares about you."

Unable to respond, Danielle took her chai latte from Chrissy and walked back out the Bistro, ignoring the stares and whispers. She was the girlfriend of an accused child predator. No wonder people couldn't stop looking at her. They probably wondered if she knew. Why hadn't he told her about this? How long had he known about the accusations?

He let her walk around town with him, arm in arm, knowing that he was accused of something horrible. How well did she really know Mark? It had only been seven weeks since she arrived in Minden. Terrible people fooled their closest friends and family for far longer than that. Danielle knew firsthand what it was like to be pressured by someone in authority. She'd never felt so cheap as when her former boss had propositioned her in the small hotel office.

Danielle could still feel his hot breath on the back of her neck and his hand above her knee. What had those young girls thought when their trusted teacher had done whatever it was that he'd done to them? She shook the mental image from her head, but it was replaced with the sweet picture of Mark kneeling down to talk to a young girl at the Fourth of July picnic. And another with the middle school girls he'd given high fives to at church one Sunday morning. At the time, she'd thought it sweet that Mark was so good with kids. Now? Every memory held suspicion.

And he was on retreat with the high schoolers! Did the church know about this? How could they let him chaperone the trip, when he was accused of this horrible thing? Danielle took a sip of her chai latte, but it was bitter in her mouth, flavored with the doubt and anger of the secret just revealed.

Unable to return to the bakery quite yet, she'd turned to walk the opposite way, toward the park. If he told her he was innocent, would she believe him? It was the word of three girls against him. Three! Wasn't that a pattern of abuse? Why would three separate girls claim something so awful?

They were brave to come forward, Danielle mused. After she told her manager and was accused of lying, she quit her job and never looked back. Leaving that job was the reason she ran out of money for culinary school. One moment in the office of an ordinary hotel had impacted the trajectory of her life for years to come. What would Mark's actions do to those poor girls?

Her stomach roiled at the thought and Dani stifled a gag, her small drink of chai threatening to make a reappearance in the bushes. She opened the lid and dumped the rest into the grass before throwing the paper cup in the nearby trashcan. She had to get back and let Aunt Maggie take a break.

As hard as she tried to focus, her mind kept wandering back to the situation at hand. Even Aunt

Maggie could tell something was wrong, but Dani couldn't bring herself to tell her. She'd find out soon enough, since Maggie was friends with Mark's mom, Donna.

That brought fresh, painful thoughts of Mark's family. They were so welcoming and kind. How would they feel, knowing their son and brother was actually a predator? Donna would be devastated. The whole family, really. And Dani was mad at Mark again for his selfishness. It wasn't just his life that he'd impacted with his actions. It was his entire family. It was her. And those girls. She didn't want to let herself forget the true victims.

While she decorated a birthday cake for a special order, Dani prayed.

God, let justice be done. Help Mark get help. I don't understand, God. I thought he loved You. Everything I know about him was a lie, God. I just don't know how I missed it. How could you let me be so wrong about him? I thought you brought me here for a reason?

Was I wrong to think he was a part of that? What was I supposed to learn from this relationship with him? And it ending like this? Obviously, it's ending. I can't be with someone like him. I'm feeling so betrayed, God. I want to yell and scream at him!

Pleas and questions received no response from God this time. Aunt Maggie walked into the kitchen, with the aid of her cane. "Okay, Dani. Tell me what's going on."

"It's nothing, Aunt Maggie." There was no emotion in her voice as Dani stared at the frosting.

"It is something," Margaret insisted. "Now, I'm going to sit here and knead this bread and you tell me about it." She uncovered the dough in a stainless-steel mixing bowl and reached for a handful of flour. Danielle watched her bony hands expertly work the dough.

"It's about Mark." She paused, almost unable to say the rest. "He's under investigation for inappropriate conduct with a student. Well, with several students."

Aunt Maggie's hands stilled. "Oh my. How did you hear about this?"

"It's all over town, apparently. I found out at the bistro." Dani recalled the whispers and stares. The judgment.

"Oh, poor Donna. I'll have to call her." Aunt Maggie started kneading again.

"I feel like such an idiot. I thought I loved him, Aunt Maggie!" Despite the cool air conditioning, Danielle's face felt warm and her throat thick.

"You thought you did? Or you did?"

She looked at her aunt, remembering sitting on the porch swing in Mark's arms. "How could I love someone who would do *that* to thirteen-year-old girls?" Regardless of what her memories told her.

"I don't think you could. Which is why I'm

asking." Margaret shrugged a shoulder. "If you love him, maybe he didn't do it."

Dani's voice rose an octave, "Three girls say differently! Why would I believe him over them? Why does every one assume a woman is lying when she tries to tell someone she's been taken advantage of?" Her voice cracked and she tried not to let tears escape. Maggie didn't know about her own experience. Danielle composed herself. "I have to believe the victims."

"I've known Mark Dawson his entire life," Aunt Maggie said quietly, almost to herself. Maggie brushed her hair from her forehead with her arm. "I know some people are capable of terrible things and manage to fool their friends and family. But I believe he's innocent."

"I wish I could." Danielle completed the bottom trim of the cake and stepped back. She grabbed another piping bag for the writing.

"Why don't you wait until the investigation is over?"

Danielle shook her head and squeezed icing onto the top of the cake. "I can't. Everyone in town is already looking at me and whispering about how I'm dating the teacher who touches students." The cake grew blurry as tears filled her vision "I get enough scrutiny on my own around here. I can't take on anymore because of him."

Aunt Maggie pressed her lips together and her

eyes closed slowly before opening and staying focused on the dough. "Alright then. It sounds like you've already decided."

Danielle blinked the tears into her shoulder and replied. "I have."

Chapter 20

Mark drove past his house slowly, dismayed to see the news van was still parked in front. His neighbors stood outside their houses, talking to each other on the sidewalk. They would recognize his car, so he ducked his head. He drove to his parents' house and pulled in the driveway; grateful no one was camped out with protest signs. After walking through the front door, he melted into his mother's waiting arms and held her tightly. It was a soothing balm on his hurt that no matter what, he was loved by his family.

"Hey, Mom."

"My sweet boy, I'm so glad you're home." She patted his back and kissed the side of his head.

"The news van is still in front of my house."

"I know." She swore in Italian. "Vampires."

Stephen, Gideon and his dad came in from the living room, avoiding his gaze and abnormally quiet.

"Hey." Mark broke the silence.

His dad spoke first, "You okay?"

"Not really." He shrugged. "What's it like in town?"

Gideon grimaced. "It's not pretty, man. The things people are saying..."

Richard interrupted, "It doesn't matter what people say. We know you didn't do this. And we *will* stand by you, son."

Mark's heart swelled and he let out a breath. "Thanks, Dad."

"What can we do?" Stephen's quiet voice was kind.

His mother spoke up. "First, we pray. Then, we eat. Come, come. Richard, would you?" His dad nodded solemnly and they circled around Mark. His father prayed, full of emotion and passion, for the truth to conquer and for strength of each member of the family. Stephen murmured agreement and hands squeezed his shoulders lightly in emphasis of his father's words. Their covering him in prayer was as natural as engulfing him in hugs and as palpable. His father's words wrapped around him. When the prayer ended and they all wiped their eyes, Mark hugged his father tightly.

"Thanks, Dad."

His dad pulled back and placed a hand on each shoulder and looked down at him, square in the eyes. "You're a good man, Mark Anthony. Anyone who says differently is wrong." Then, Richard pulled him close again.

Dinner was subdued; their typical rambunctious stories and good-natured ribbing was conspicuously absent. The raviolo was delicious, but sat heavily in his stomach. Mark caught his mother watching him more than once and tried his best to eat. He hadn't eaten at all today, but still found it difficult to swallow each bite. He'd checked his phone a dozen times on the drive, but there was nothing from Danielle. Why hadn't she reached out?

"What should I do?" The question sounded simple, but the reality of the situation wasn't. He looked around the table at his parents and brothers. "How do I show my face around town?"

His mom took a drink, and Gideon wiped his mouth. Finally, Stephen spoke up. "You've got to stand up and tell the world your side of the story."

"What story? I have no idea what these girls are talking about! I never did anything wrong!" Agitation rose again at the familiar narrative.

"Then that's what you have to say. But, the longer you are quiet, the more people will fill in the blanks themselves." Stephen was smart and thoughtful. Other than Malachi, he was the most logical thinker of the group. "Go to your house, get the attention of the news van and give a statement." Stephen checked his watch. "If you go soon, you might be able to have your statement as part of the story on the nine o'clock news. We'll all go and stand beside you. A show of support."

Mark considered it. The last thing he wanted to do was stand in front of a crowd who already thought he was guilty. They'd dismiss his denial, wouldn't they? Why would they believe him? But what was the alternative? Letting people believe he was guilty?

Mark stepped away from the table and tried to call Danielle. When her voicemail picked up, he left a message. "Hey, Dani. I really need to talk to you. I'm sure you've heard some really terrible things. I just want a chance to explain. Please, call me back." Then, he started thinking about what he would say when the cameras were on him.

His family finished their dinner and they loaded in his parent's SUV. It was almost like being a kid again, the three of them squeezed in the backseat and arguing about which seatbelt belonged to who. Instead of the normal Christian radio station, the ride was silent.

When they pulled up, Mark saw the crowd of bystanders on the sidewalk. Mostly unfamiliar faces, plus some he recognized from parent-teacher conferences. They didn't look friendly. He almost told his dad to go back home. Then, on the other side of the news van; there was another group. Luke and Charlotte, Ruth and Norman, and Todd and Chrissy. Several others, close friends from the men's ministry at church. Mark scanned the crowd for any sight of Danielle, but he couldn't spot her curly brown hair in the group. Tucking away his disappointment; he focused on the friends who'd come. Mark looked at Stephen. "What did you do?"

"Your family is behind you for this. All of us. I just sent word to Luke, and he did the rest." Mark leaned forward and hugged his brother, awkwardly straining against the seatbelt still pinning him in place.

"Thank you. I'm sorry I didn't tell you before."

"Hey, it's okay. I wish you would have, but I understand." Stephen patted him on the back. They unbuckled and opened the door. "Are you ready for this?"

"As ready as I'll ever be, I guess."

He greeted the small group of supporters with hugs and grateful smiles and then made his way toward the news camera. The reporter eagerly got the attention of her camera man and began battering him with questions. "Mr. Dawson, are you guilty? What do you have to say for yourself? How many girls have you assaulted?" She pressed toward him and Gideon, with his large frame stepped between them.

"My brother will make a statement for the record in a moment. Just make sure your cameras are rolling."

"Mr. Dawson, have you ever been accused of improper conduct before? Did the school cover up your crimes?"

Again, Gideon intervened. "Ma'am, please step back." He looked down at the grass of Mark's front yard where they were now walking. "You are trespassing on private property."

The reporter looked down and realized she had left the public sidewalk. With a flip of her blond hair, she turned and walked back, whispering to her camera man and pulling out her cellphone.

Mark laid a hand on his brother's shoulder. "Thanks, bro."

"Anytime. Journalists are the worst." Gideon gave a sarcastic smile and Mark couldn't help but laugh at his brothers self-deprecating humor. Oh, it felt good to laugh. The reporter's excitement had stirred the attention of the crowd protesting on the sidewalk.

Insults were hurled in his direction and Mark closed his eyes. Praying for the words he needed, and the strength to turn the other cheek, he stepped onto the porch steps of his small bungalow and raised a hand.

"Please-"

"Scum!"

"You should be in jail!"

Mark held up both hands. "Please. I know you're upset." The crowd quieted and the attention was on him. A giant spotlight turned on, obscuring the reporter and her microphone from his view. But he knew it was pointed at him. "I know you're upset, and you have every right to be. The thought that someone in your child's school would take advantage of your children is sickening." Mark swallowed heavily. "I was notified in early June I was being investigated for what they called inappropriate contact."

Murmurs rose within the crowd and Mark raised his voice over them. "These allegations are unequivocally false! I have no doubt I will be exonerated during the course of the investigation," he stated firmly. Then, his voice softened, "It is my understanding that three female students are making the claim. I have no idea why they would target me with these malicious lies, but that is what they are: lies. In my eight years as a teacher, I have prided myself in caring for your students, teaching them and setting a godly example for them."

Emotion filled his voice. "I love being a teacher. I would never do anything to jeopardize that. More than that, though, I call myself a Christian and a man of my word. We live in a world where terrible things happen, and innocent children are victims of abuse far too often. With a male teacher, it is easy to see ulterior motives where there are none. I teach because I love to teach and because I want to make a difference for every student who sits at a desk in my classroom."

Mark looked directly into the camera. "To the girls who've made up this story: it's not too late to tell the truth. Your lies could ruin an innocent man." Then, looking toward the crowd. "To everyone else, I ask you to consider my innocence a possibility before you condemn me in the court of public opinion. Join me," he gestured to his family, "and my family, in praying the truth will come to light. We can all agree that is the best outcome."

The reporter peppered him with questions and Mark waved her off as he walked back to his parents' vehicle. As he was about to climb in, Mark turned back toward the crowd of bystanders. A familiar glimpse of light brown skin and curly brown hair caught his eye, but Danielle offered no smile. There was no glimmer of recognition or friendship as his eyes met hers. He watched, helplessly, as she turned and walked the opposite direction. It was a statement as plain and clear as the one he just finished making. No words necessary. Dani wasn't on his side. Mark rubbed his chest at the stab of pain and climbed into the car with Stephen following close behind.

Gideon was exchanging heated words with the young, fiery reporter, but when he finished, Gideon walked to the other side and sat beside Mark. Despite being surrounded by his brothers and his parents; all Mark could focus on was the one person he'd needed to stand beside him. And she had refused. A dozen of his closest friends stood beside him as he proclaimed his innocence. But Danielle walked away without a glance. The memory made him press his lips together. The image of her turning her back on him relived with fresh waves of pain and betrayal the entire ride back to his childhood home.

Chapter 21

Danielle watched from the safety of the crowd as Mark gave his press conference. She had to admit, his words rang true. The emotion in his voice, pleading for the truth made her want to run to him. But she'd seen too many guilty men proclaim their innocence with absolute fervor. It was easier to just be done. Danielle decided she would stay the rest of the week. Then, when she went to California for the wedding, she could decide whether to come back. Aunt Maggie was doing okay, the in-home therapy was helping tremendously. But it would still be months before her aunt would be able to take over running the bakery, if at all.

As much as Danielle wanted to stay and run the bakery; she couldn't see living here with Mark just around the corner. How did people live in small towns, anyway? Every ex-boyfriend lived five blocks away! At least in California, she could avoid them forever if she wanted to. Here, Danielle would see him constantly. And even if he left after the investigation, she'd still run into his mom and his brothers - reminding her how close they'd been and the hurt of finding out about the real him.

But why should she give up her dream because he had screwed up? Danielle loved running the bakery. By all accounts, she was quite good at it. There was so much freedom and satisfaction in being the one in charge. Aunt Maggie had a solid business built here. It would be difficult to replicate in California, where there was competition on every block. When Dani finally talked about it with Aunt Maggie, her aunt's calm response was a stark contrast to the whirlwind of thoughts inside her own head.

"I understand, dearie. If it's too hard to stay, you just go ahead and go back to California." Aunt Maggie laid a thin hand on Dani's cheek and patted it softly. "It was a gift to just have you here and be able to make things right."

"What will you do with the bakery?"

"Oh, I don't know. I suppose I'll have to sell it." Maggie's tone was matter-of-fact. "I couldn't keep up with things alone, and even with a bit of hourly help I think I'd wear myself ragged."

"I hate to make you give it up."

"Now, now. Don't you worry about me. I was never foolish enough to believe I'd get to keep it forever."

Dani's constitution wavered. "Well, I'm not sure yet. I'll come back after the wedding and stay until the end of August at least. It will give you some time. I can survive four more weeks in Minden," she conceded.

Dani managed to avoid Mark the rest of the week; he wasn't venturing out too much anyway. Gideon stopped her one morning at the Bistro, though. "Where have you been, Dani?" Gideon towered over her, his voice rough and accusing.

"Look, I'm not doing this." Danielle shook her head and waited for him to move.

"What do you mean, you aren't doing this? He loved you! And you just totally bail on him?" Gideon waved his hands wildly and his volume increased with each sentence.

The stares of other customers were hot on her neck. "Gideon, please." She stepped to one side and he mirrored her action, still blocking her way.

He crossed his arms. "You know what, Dani? Mark deserves someone who will stand by him. When he's found innocent, don't expect to come running back to him. You're not good for him."

Danielle lowered her shoulder and ducked around Gideon's large frame, escaping out the door. She wiped away the unexpected sting of hot tears behind her eyes. *I'm not good enough for him? He's the one accused of abusing a student!* But the familiar words hit too close to home. Never good enough.

*****

Dani sat next to the empty seat on the nonstop flight from Indianapolis to San Francisco. Without Mark, the extended weekend trip seemed like a waste, but she resolved to make the most of it. They'd been planning to stay with Malachi, so Dani texted Casey about crashing at her place. But Casey was already out in Napa - as the maid of honor, she was with Adele helping with all the last-minute details. Dani asked Liz next and rejoiced when Liz said she had space and they could attend the wedding together.

Danielle retrieved her bags and prepared to find a taxi when she glanced at the row of professional drivers holding signs for their expected passengers. One read "Mark Dawson and Danielle Washington". *Oh, great. Mark didn't tell his brother we weren't coming.* Dani wheeled her suitcase over to the older man dressed in a crisp black suit.

"Um, hi. I'm Danielle Washington."

"Excellent. My name is Arthur, ma'am." Arthur immediately reached for her suitcase and she pulled it away from his reach.

"Actually, I just wanted to let you know your services will not be needed."

"Pardon me, ma'am. Mr. Dawson arranged for this car."

Danielle rolled her eyes. "I figured. But his brother did not come with me. Therefore, no car." She started to walk toward the taxi line.

"Ma'am, it's already been paid for. Non-refundable. I'm sure even if Mr. Dawson, Mark Dawson, that is, couldn't come with you, they would still want you to use the services."

"Somehow, I doubt it." Still, if it was paid for? A cab from the airport to Liz's house would cost her fifty or sixty bucks she really didn't have. "Okay, fine. But only because it's already paid for."

This time, Arthur reached for her suitcase and Dani let him take it. Then, she followed him to a line of black town cars and slid into the cool, dark interior when Arthur opened the door. *This is way better than a dingy cab.*

"May I offer you a water, ma'am?" Arthur turned slightly from the front seat and held out a bottle of imported water. Danielle untwisted the top and took a sip.

"Thanks, Arthur."

"My pleasure, ma'am."

"Hey, Arthur?" She caught his eye in the mirror.

"Yes, ma'am?"

"Stop calling me ma'am."

"Yes ma'am." His smile flashed.

"Here's the address." She handed him a piece of paper with Liz's address on it.

"Oh, are you staying with Miss Hunter?"

"Liz? Yes. How do you know her?"

"I've driven her home many times for Mr. Dawson."

Interesting. "Hmm. Well, I guess that means you know where we're going, then."

"Yes, ma'am."

"Arthur!" she said, teasing him.

Arthur ducked his head. "My apologies, Miss Washington."

"It's Dani."

"Okay, Dani."

They pulled up in front of a tall building, and Arthur walked around to let Dani out. He handed her suitcase to her and she thanked him. "I hope you enjoy your time in San Francisco, Dani."

"Thanks, Arthur. I appreciate the ride."

The doorman checked her name and let her inside the building. Apparently, Liz was doing okay for herself, she pondered. Danielle had never been to her condo before. Knit Night was always at Adele's place. They'd been friends for a while, but they mostly hung out in groups. When she knocked on Liz's door, Liz opened it quickly and welcomed her inside.

"Come in, come in! I'm so sorry I couldn't pick

you up from the airport myself, but I just got home from work. Besides, Malachi's assistant told me he arranged a car for you guys."

"Oh, I thought Malachi had done it. I figured he would cancel it once he knew Mark wasn't coming."

Liz waved a hand. "I'd be surprised if he even remembered today was the day you were supposed to arrive. Malachi lives in his own world. Don't get me wrong, he's brilliant. But a bit distracted. Especially right now, he's all tied up in this project he's got going. I haven't seen him in days."

"Really? That's bizarre." The mystery of Mark's brother was becoming more and more interesting.

Liz shrugged. "Not really. He tends to disappear when he's onto something. Either way, I'm not even sure he knows what's going on with Mark or if he would have thought about the changes to your plans. So here we are!"

"Thanks so much for letting me stay here. I couldn't spring for a hotel and the flights were already booked for the earlier dates."

Liz guided her through the house and stopped to grab them each a bottle of water. "It's no problem, seriously. I'm just glad to have someone to drive up to the wedding with me. Malachi is supposed to go, I assume. But who knows if he'll show up? And I would rather not ride with my boss anyway, you know?"

Dani accepted the water and nodded. "Of

course. Well, don't interrupt your routine for me. Just act like I'm not here."

"Whatever!" Liz scoffed. "It's been ages; we have so much to catch up on! I took a half day off. So, let's go do something."

"Like what?"

Liz pursed her lips to one side, thinking. "Well... I need a dress for the wedding. Should we go shopping?" She guided Dani into the guest bedroom and laid the suitcase on a bench.

"Sure. I haven't been shopping in ages. There aren't exactly a ton of stores in Minden. Besides, I'm mostly jeans and t-shirts, you know?"

"What are you wearing to the wedding?"

"Oh, just a sundress." Danielle unzipped her suitcase and pulled the now wrinkly and pathetic-looking fabric from her bag. The simple, yellow sundress had seen better days.

Liz looked at the dress balefully. "Nope." She shook her head. "I'm sure you would look great in it, but we are going shopping and we are going to get new dresses so we look amazing in all the pictures of the wedding!"

"Liz, I really-" Dani tried to interrupt her friend's excitement.

"Come on, now. My treat. I can put my recent bonus to good use."

Danielle was shaking her head. It was one thing to accept the ride from Malachi, but charity from her friend? "I can't."

"Please? This weekend is going to be hard enough - I hate going to weddings without a date. Please let me play fairy godmother and get us both looking fabulous?" Liz pushed out her lower lip and gave Dani a puppy-dog begging face.

Dani sighed. "Fine, let's go shopping." Liz beamed and clapped her hands together. "But," Dani held up a finger, "I'm helping pay for the dress." She didn't know what money she would use. Maggie had given her a paycheck for the weeks of work at the bakery, but most had already gone to paying off the credit cards she'd maxed out to travel to Indiana.

Dani and Liz went shopping and hit several boutique clothing stores in a trendy, upscale district of San Francisco. Danielle could never have afforded to shop there, and she tugged on her "Bookmarks are for quitters" T-shirt, feeling out of place. Liz was in her element though, and the shopkeepers responded to her obvious confidence. In the end, they picked a dark blue floral cocktail dress for Liz, fitted just enough to give Liz's tall, lean frame a hint of curves.

Liz latched on to a pale pink, glittery fit-and-flare dress for Dani. "Please, please, just try it on." Finally, Danielle relented and took the sparkling dress into the fitting room. It was so far from her comfort zone, Dani thought she might need a map to get back. But she put it on and looked in the mirror. Her cheeks went pink and she lifted her chin. A lightness in her chest accompanied a wide smile. The dress was perfect. Not too tight, but not baggy, either. It swished around her knees and shimmered in the fluorescent lights. The color contrasted against her skin, making it appear warm and glowy.

"Come show me!" she heard Liz call from outside the fitting room. Danielle took a deep breath and opened the door. "Holy smokes, girl! It's amazing on you. You look like a million bucks!"

Danielle laughed and swished her hips, making the dress dance around her knees. "Not a million bucks, just-" she checked the tag pinned at her hip and choked. "Gah-six hundred?" She'd never worn anything so expensive in her entire life. Visions of spilling wine on the dress filled her head. "I have to get this off."

"Not so fast. This dress was made for you. I'm buying it."

"I can't let-"

"Yes, you can, Dani. You've had a rough summer. You lost your job. You lost your car and your apartment. And I never once heard you complain. You went halfway across the country to help an aunt you barely even knew. And you lived in the smallest town known to man." Danielle snorted a laugh. After laying a hand on Danielle's bare shoulder, Liz continued, "and you fell in love. And then you found out he might be a monster, which broke your heart." The last words were tender and soft, but now Liz straightened up and said with sass, "So girl, if anybody needs retail therapy right now - it's you."

Chapter 22

Adele had really outdone herself; the wedding was incredible. As Dani and Liz were escorted to their seats, a string quartet provided soft music. The seats and altar were in the grass overlooking hills filled with grape vines. The lush green of the vineyard stretched for miles. Countless uniform rows of grapes winding through the hills and valleys. The centerpiece of the altar was a wrought iron arch decked out with flowers and delicately draped ivory chiffon.

They sat on the white, wooden folding chairs waiting for the ceremony to begin. Casey's purple bridesmaid's dress popped against fresh white flowers of the bouquet. Casey was followed down the aisle by an adorable little flower girl tossing rose petals as high as she could and giggling with every handful. Then Adele, in a gorgeous ivory lace wedding dress. Dani stole a glance at Calvin when Adele made her appearance and his beaming smile and subtle swipe at a tear told her everything she needed to know.

Liz and Dani dried their eyes with crumpled tissues as they watched their friend declare her love. Adele radiated joy, and Calvin wore a soft, awed smile through the entire ceremony; as though he couldn't believe he was this lucky.

The reception took place under a large tent on the other side of the winery grounds. Liz and Danielle found their table and Liz set down her clutch before offering to get them each a drink from one of several bars set up in the tent. Danielle pursed her lips at the empty seat with a place card for Mark Dawson. Beside it, the name Malachi Dawson in elegant script. *Oh, please let him still be in whatever crazy inventor cave he's been hiding in.* No such luck, though, and a handsome man with familiar features pulled out the chair. Dani could see Richard's large football-player physique in Malachi, despite his tendency toward academics instead of athletics. He had the same dark Italian hair and eyes as Mark. When he looked at her, she couldn't help but see Mark's eyes boring into hers after his press conference.

"You must be Danielle. I've heard a lot about

you." Malachi's voice was rough, his speech slightly awkward and stilted. Every word was measured.

"Umm, hi. Yes, I'm Danielle. It's-" *awkward, so awkward,* she sang internally. But she finished, "nice to meet you, Malachi."

"I was disappointed to hear my brother would not be attending. I was looking forward to seeing him." Malachi spoke so formally; it was slightly disconcerting. "It has been too long."

"Yes, well." Dani wished for a hole to open up and swallow her. "I'm sure you also heard we broke up."

"I do believe my mother mentioned you had not been around since..." he trailed off, circling a hand in the air.

"Right. Since." She agreed flatly. Leave it to him to bring up the elephant at the table.

"Well, I do not wish to ruin your evening. Despite your history with my brother, I am simply here to celebrate the wedding of my good friend, Calvin and his lovely bride." He raised a glass in their direction. To Danielle's immense relief, Liz returned to the table with two glasses of champagne. "Ah, Liz. What a surprise. I did not realize you would be here. Have you become friends with Calvin through our dealings?"

"Actually, Mr. Dawson, Adele is a great friend of mine. I believe I've mentioned that on several occasions." Liz's irritation with her boss was restrained, but definitely present. Even Liz's tone was different; mirroring the formal inflection of Malachi's.

"Ah, yes. Of course." Malachi's distracted response made it clear he had no idea what Liz was talking about. Liz mentioned he lived in his own world, but yikes. *He's aware of the situation in Minden, so he must not be totally isolated,* Danielle mused.

The conversation turned to pleasantries: the ceremony, the weather, and the beautiful scenery. Other guests joined them at their table and dinner was served. Danielle was served a vegetarian entree, already pre-arranged. *Adele never misses a detail.* The giant stuffed portobello mushroom looked fantastic and Dani was eager to dig in. Liz's salmon smelled like fresh lemon and rosemary and Danielle tried to avoid looking at the juice running across Malachi's plate as he cut into his pink steak.

Danielle sipped her champagne and listened to the band while the conversation went on around her. Clearly, she and Mark had been seated at the table because of Liz and Malachi. But as a result, the rest of the guests were also business contacts of Calvin and the conversation, coupled with the alcohol, threatened to put Danielle to sleep.

After Calvin and Adele shared their first dance and fed each other cake - she recognized Casey's salted caramel crunch cupcake - the dance floor was open. Malachi stood and laid his napkin on the back of his chair. He held out a hand to Danielle. "May I have this dance?"

Danielle was sure her mouth was hanging open like a fish out of water, lips wavering as she tried to process. He should hate her, right? Giving up on trying to make sense of it, she placed her hand in his and they walked to the dance floor. Malachi was tall; much taller than his brother. Despite the three-inch heels Liz lent her, she barely reached his shoulder. The band played a familiar song-a classic by Nat King Cole-and they swayed gently along. Malachi spoke first. Danielle was still struggling to understand why he was being so kind to her after she'd bailed on his brother.

"It must have been hard for you." He tipped his head down to direct his words toward her ear, speaking quietly so only she could hear.

"What?"

"It must have been hard. Hearing the news that your boyfriend might have done something terrible to some innocent students. I mean," he continued, "it is obviously hard for our family. But you did not know him well."

"Just well enough to feel duped," she confirmed. Malachi was insightful, she'd give him that.

"Yes, well, I am sorry."

She sighed and let him twirl her. When she was

close again; she spoke. "It's my own fault. I thought I knew him."

"Perhaps you did," he said simply.

"I don't think so. If I'd known him, I would have known about the investigation. Before it was on the news."

"Maybe so," he conceded. "But can you blame a man for not wanting the woman he loves to look at him with doubt in her eyes?"

"Honestly, I can. And I do." Who else was there to blame? Mark had kept the secret. Mark had seduced students.

It was Malachi's turn to sigh. "You are not afraid to say what you think, are you?"

"Not usually." She wasn't going to be loud or in-your-face with her opinion, but she knew what she thought and wasn't ashamed of it. Her mother had given her the confidence to stand strong.

"Well, then, do you mind if I do the same?"

"Feel free." Danielle was curious. Unlike Gideon, Malachi was soft-spoken and deliberate. He'd orchestrated every moment of this dance in order to have this conversation.

"Okay. Here is what I think. I think Mark is innocent." Dani started to pull away, but he gave a gentle tug on her hand. "Please, Ms. Washington. Hear me out." She relented and placed her other hand once more on his shoulder. "I think he is innocent. I think you were hurt he chose not to confide in you, and I think you were appalled at the possibility your judgment was so skewed." They barely swayed now. "And here is what I know: I know he still loves you. More than that; I know he loves God. I *think* you still love him too." He stepped away and looked her in the eyes. "And I *think* if you let him go without a fight, you will regret it for the rest of your life." Then, Malachi gave a gentle bow and walked back to their table, leaving her alone in the center of the dance floor. Couples swayed around her and the final notes of "Unforgettable" hung in the air.

*****

Malachi danced with Liz once and then made his excuses and left. "I hope I will see you again, Ms. Washington. Please, think about what I said."

Danielle nodded, highly aware she'd been thinking of nothing else but what he said during their brief dance. Could Mark still love her? Even crazier, did she still love him? With the cloud of the accusations hanging over him? Mark had never done anything to make her doubt him, except for keeping the investigation a secret from her. Was her reaction simply whiplash? They'd gone from declarations of love on a blanket alone under the stars to unspoken conversations on the sidewalk in an angry crowd.

Where was the root of her adamant acceptance of the students' claims? Did she really believe them because the accusations rang true? She recalled the scarce details she knew. Three girls. Mark. Inappropriate contact. Her own story had been true and dismissed anyway. But it was dismissed by a disinterested manager more concerned about having to hire a replacement supervisor than about uncovering truth. The manager didn't know the supervisor's heart. Did she know Mark's heart? Did his story ring true, when she set aside the emotion of her own experience?

All Dani had ever wanted was to be accepted. To be judged for more than what was on the surface. And yet, when given the opportunity to prove she valued more than the surface-level appearance of Mark, she'd bailed. Gideon was right. Mark deserved better. He deserved someone who would stand by him and believe in him. Someone who would see the true man behind the trendy shoes and styled hair and comic book collection. Danielle had seen that man, and God help her, she loved him. And she loved him still.

Danielle had to get back to Indiana and tell Mark. Before the investigation proved his innocence, she had to let him know she had his back. That she saw him and loved him. And believed him.

Adele and Calvin came up to their table; making

the rounds to greet all their guests.

"Congratulations!" Dani hugged Adele and introduced herself to Calvin. "I'm so happy for you."

"I'm so glad you were able to come! Where is Mark?" Dani hadn't had a chance to tell anyone except Liz about the investigation.

"Actually, it's a long story. But the important thing is that I need to get back to Indiana as soon as possible. I messed up big time and I have to fix it." She gave a grimace. "But... my flight isn't until Tuesday!" She hadn't thought about it until now. The whole investigation could be over by then. And she'd look like the fair-weather friend.

Calvin spoke up, with his arm around his bride. "Take the jet."

Liz, Adele, and Danielle spoke in unison, "What?"

Calvin opened a palm. "My helicopter is waiting to take us to the airport. Ride with us back to the city and then take the jet. My pilot can drop you off and then come back for us. We're headed to Hawaii, so Indiana isn't exactly on the way, or I'd say we'd just let you hitch a ride with us." He winked and Danielle's heart melted at his kindness.

Instead of addressing the incredibly generous man in front of her, she looked at Adele. Her friend was smiling dreamily up at her new husband. "Adele?"

"I'm sure we can find something to do with an extra night in San Francisco." Adele's comment made herself blush and Calvin cleared his throat.

"Yes, I'm sure that won't be an issue. Please, we insist." He smiled broadly. "Love is patient, but that doesn't mean we can't help move things along."

Dani raised an eyebrow. "Okay, Adele. I thought you said he was intimidating?" Danielle thought back to the stories about Calvin over the years while Adele was his assistant.

Adele threw her head back and laughed. "Truth is, you've missed a few things while you've been gone. Turns out, he just needed a little chocolate fix to loosen him up."

Chapter 23

Mark felt like a prisoner. His own home was egged and someone had spray-painted nasty words on his front porch. He was staying at his parents' house, but he feared it was only a matter of time until they were targeted as well. It seemed the entire community had turned on him. His closest friends maintained their belief in his innocence, but everyone else in the tri-county area seemed to have already decided he was guilty. It wasn't like he could blame them, either. It was hard to argue with three separate claims from students.

Mark tried to escape through video games, but even chatting with his online friends couldn't clear his head. He missed Danielle. She was at the wedding this weekend. The wedding he was supposed to attend. Malachi had been tagged in some pictures from the wedding, and he spotted Danielle wearing a knock-out dress.

Wow.

He gritted his teeth in frustration at seeing her dancing with Malachi, knowing it should have been him instead. Mark was still studying the picture when his mom walked into the room he had once shared with Malachi. In some ways, he felt like he was fourteen again. Everything was completely turbulent and there was nothing he could do. He was trying his best to trust God was in control. Unfortunately, it felt trite and untrue in face of such daunting trials.

God, I want to believe you have this all under control. You've got a plan in this, right? With everything falling out from under him, Mark clung even more to the promises of God. *I love you. And I know you work all things together for good.*

"Hey, sweetie. It's almost noon." His mom was dressed up, apparently just back from church. "Don't you think you should come eat something?"

"Not hungry," he mumbled. He clicked to the next picture. The bride and groom were feeding each other cake. He rolled his eyes, but clicked to the next picture anyway, searching for any glimpse of Danielle or Malachi.

"*Marco*, please?" his mother pleaded. At her concerned voice, he closed his eyes. This was hard on her as much as him, he figured. No doubt church had been a discipline in biting her tongue, something his hot-blooded Italian mother was never very good at.

He stood. "Sorry, Mom. I'll come down now."

"Thank you. I'm worried about you."

"I'll be okay." Even as he said the words, he doubted their veracity. How could he be okay? Was this how David felt, hiding in the caves, just waiting for the enemy to discover him? Any day now, Steve would call and tell him he was fired. Probably criminal charges next. He didn't really know. But he was holed up here, just waiting the inevitable. Danielle wanted nothing to do with him. Fellow teachers were undoubtedly whispering about him while getting their classrooms ready for the new school year. The parents at church and school were blaming themselves for not seeing the monster in their midst.

And here he was. Playing video games and pathetically stalking pictures of his ex-girlfriend online. Irritated with his brother for getting to dance with her. *Traitor.* Mark followed his mother down the stairs and froze on the bottom step.

There, in the kitchen, stood Danielle. Still in the glittering pink dress he saw in pictures, she stood barefoot with heels hanging from one hand. Shock was replaced with hot rage and he tried to turn around in retreat up the stairs. Mark stumbled and fell, catching himself on his forearms on the fourth step up. *Why was she here?* He hung he head and gently beat his head against the edge of the step. His body couldn't take one more blow, it seemed, and seeing Danielle? That was the mother of all punches. Mark turned and sat on the step, hands clasped and forearms on his knees. Fists clenched, he spoke through a tight jaw.

"Get out." Danielle took a step toward him and he held up a hand. "I said, get out."

"Please, Mark. Listen to me."

"If you had something to say, you should have said it a week ago." Mark pointed to the door. She'd left him before. And it had nearly killed him to watch her go.

"I wasn't ready then. But I am now."

"Oh, great. You're ready now. Well, I'm not." Mark stood, the steps giving him a healthy height advantage. Looking down on her, he asked "Do you know how much it hurt? I tried calling. I tried showing up. You wouldn't answer. You wouldn't see me. What was I supposed to think?" He closed his eyes, reliving the moment he watched her turn her back on him.

Danielle hung her head. "I'm so sorry. I should have-"

"You're right. You should have given your boyfriend a chance." Mark shook his head. "I *loved* you, Dani."

"Darn it, Mark! Don't you see it was hard for

me? I heard *from Chrissy* that the man I love was accused of something too horrible to think about?" Danielle stepped closer, looking up at him. Her golden-brown eyes pleaded with him. "I was scared. Suddenly, I was the object of whispers, just as much as you. I was afraid it was true." He flinched at the words. He'd known that was the case, but hearing her say it was salt on the wound.

She reached out and tried to touch his arm. Mark pulled away further and saw the hurt register in her gaze. "I know it isn't, now. But at first? It was easy to believe the reason you didn't tell me was because it was true!" She took a deep breath. "And even if you can't forgive me, I'm sorry I doubted you. Even for a moment." She turned around and picked up the heels where she'd dropped them on the tile floor. "I'll pray for the truth, Mark."

With that, she headed for the door. Mark watched, unable to move. His feet were rooted firmly to the worn stair tread. Danielle thought he was a monster. Her admission felt like a knife to the gut. Out of all the angry messages and disgusted looks he received in the last week, Danielle's hurt the most. How could he forgive her for that? *Can I forgive her?* The door slammed in its frame, marking Danielle's exit. Again. This time it wasn't her choice to leave, though. He'd forced her out. For some reason, it didn't hurt any less. *Oh, God. What am I doing?* If Danielle wanted to stand by him, isn't that what he wanted? Isn't that what he'd been desperate for only days ago?

His gaze shifted to the floor. He considered what she said. It was hard for her. The selfish part of him wanted to scoff. *Hard for you? I'm the one accused of seducing students!* Then he considered what he knew of Danielle. Despite everything about her screaming "I'm different!", she'd only ever wanted to remain unnoticed. And then the news broke and she was the center of attention as much as he. Could he blame her for running scared? Yet, she was here. The accusations still lingered, unresolved. And she'd come back. He looked up at the empty doorway, then back up the stairs to his childhood bedroom. Back to the front door. He hesitated.

His mother, father, and Gideon stood quietly off to the side during the whole exchange. Now, though, his dad spoke up. "What are you doing, son? Go get her!" Mark jolted from his trance and jogged toward the door. He was still in Star Wars pajama pants. Danielle was on the sidewalk in front of the neighbor's house, walking gingerly in her bare feet back toward her aunt's street. His feet padded softly on the concrete, tiny rocks digging into his soles as he caught up to her. She turned at the noise and her cheeks revealed smudged mascara and shiny tracks of tears.

"Don't cry." Then softer, "Please, don't cry."

She sniffed. "I'm so sorry, Mark."

"No, I'm the one who should be apologizing. I should have told you sooner. I knew I needed to tell you, but I was afraid of what you might think." He shook his head. "That, well, you would turn your back on me," he admitted.

A sob escaped from Dani's lips. "Oh Mark. And that's just what I did, isn't it? I knew better. Even as I tried to convince myself you were guilty," she looked up at him, tears in her eyes, "I knew you'd never do what they said."

"What if they find me guilty?" Mark had to ask. It was still a very real possibility.

Danielle shook her head. "They won't."

He insisted. "But what if they do?"

"Then we'll work it out. You can teach online. Or work at the bakery with me."

"The bakery? Does that mean you're staying?" A glimmer of hope dangled in front of him.

She nodded. "Yeah, it does. I've got a life here now. Even if you can't forgive me, I've got friends. And I don't want to leave Aunt Maggie. She's the only family I've got."

"I thought you hated me."

Dani shook her head. "I wanted to. I've seen too many men use their position to take what doesn't belong to them. I took my anger at them out on you. I do believe you. And the next time you have a press conference, I want to be standing there right beside you."

Mark's heart leapt. "Really?"

"Really."

He placed his hands on her bare shoulders, "I love you, Danielle."

A glance at his pajamas and she gave her best Yoda impression. "Love you, too, I do."

He laughed for the first time in a week and wrapped his arms around her. He spun in a circle, her skirt flapping around them. She threw her head back and let out a yell. When he set her down, he held her close and she wrapped her arms around his waist.

"Are you sure you want to do this?"

She looked up at him. "I'm sure. Whatever happens, I love you. And I want to be with you."

"Even if people think I abused students?"

"Even then," she confirmed. "I keep having to remind myself, it doesn't matter what people think. God knows your heart."

"I think I might need that reminder pretty often myself."

"How often?"

"I'm thinking every day for the rest of our lives ought to do it." Then, he leaned in and touched his lips to hers, still smiling.

*****

When they walked back in the house, Mark's

mother and father cheered at the sight of their clasped hands. Gideon shook his head and walked up the stairs without a word. Dani watched Mark raise an eyebrow at his mother in question, but Donna just shrugged. Danielle flashed back to her conversation with Gideon at the bistro.

"Let me talk to him," she told Mark, with a brief kiss on the cheek. He released her hand and she walked lightly up the narrow staircase. She hadn't been upstairs before, so she walked slowly; ducking her head into each room before moving to the next. At the end of the hall, she found Gideon in a small guest room. There was a tiny desk and bookshelves on one wall, a twin bed with posters hanging over it. Gideon stood in front of the window, arms crossed and looking out on the backyard. "You were right," she said, when she was standing next to him.

He turned, his imposing frame suddenly in her space. "He deserves better."

She nodded. "You're probably right. He does. We both made mistakes. And we've both forgiven each other." Gideon simply shook his head and she continued. "I met Malachi yesterday. He's a pretty smart guy. A lot like you, probably. He told me if I didn't come back and make things right with Mark, I'd regret it for the rest of my life." She gave a half-hearted laugh. "And he was right. I've made a lot of mistakes. My worries about what other people thought about me shaped too many decisions in my life." She paused a moment, then spoke firmly. "I won't let what you think about me shape this one. I love your brother."

Gideon ran a hand through his short hair. "I don't want to see Mark get hurt."

"I don't either." She laid a hand on his forearm. "I won't make the same mistake again."

Gideon gave a curt nod of acceptance. Danielle returned downstairs where Donna was already preparing lunch and when Gideon came down a few minutes later, he hugged Mark and laid a warm hand on Dani's shoulder. "I'm happy for you, bro."

"Thanks, Gideon."

"I've got some other news, also." He spoke a bit louder, gathering the attention of everyone in the kitchen. "For the past week, I've been doing some digging of my own. Once I knew who leaked the story, I was able to get the name of the girls who made the claims."

Mark dropped the dishtowel on the counter. "You did?"

"Who was it?" Donna asked.

Gideon pulled a small spiral notebook from his back pocket and read, "Morgan Witham, Brittany Taylor, and Lydia Daley."

The names meant nothing to Danielle, but she saw wheels churning behind Mark's eyes. "What? What is it? Does that mean something?"

Mark shook his head. "Not really. I know them

all, of course. They were in my classes. But other than that? Brittany was my student aide..." his voice trailed off and he closed his eyes as his body shrunk into a sigh. "I can't believe she would do that. But I think I might actually know why."

Chapter 24

Mark and Gideon talked through the afternoon. Mark explained how Brittany had dropped the ball at the end of the school year, nearly failing her final project and winding up with a C in the class. It was definitely out of the ordinary for her, since she was normally a straight-A student. She had also skipped her teacher aide period the last days of school. The other two girls had done fine in his classes, and unfortunately, he had no explanation for their vendetta.

The names of his accusers weren't public yet, but Gideon explained he guilted the information out of the secretary who leaked the information to the press to begin with. He told Mark he was going to do some more digging and left before dinner. But Mark didn't have any more information. Gideon was acting like a real-life investigator, cultivating sources and interviewing witnesses. It was fun to watch, Mark had to admit. *Other than the whole my-entire-future-on-the-line part.*

Danielle offered to play video games, but Mark was tired of them after a week locked up at his parents. Instead, they played board games, even teaching Donna and Richard how to play a complicated strategy game. The few hours of normalcy were a welcome reprieve. The last week had been a mental marathon of depressing what-if scenarios. But watching Danielle tease his father and convincing him to steal a card from someone else instead of her, Mark felt like everything would be okay.

Gideon came through the back door, letting it slam behind him. Donna gave a half-hearted "Gideon!" at the noise, but the expression on his face was one of exuberant joy.

"Oh man, I'm so amped up right now. This is awesome."

"What? What is going on?" Mark stood and Gideon walked over to him.

"I was born to be a journalist. The truth shall set you free, man! Whoooo!" Gideon pumped a fist into the air and grabbed an apple from the bowl on the kitchen counter before leaning against it and taking a bite.

"What are you talking about?"

"Tomorrow. It's going to blow your mind."

"Seriously? We have to wait until tomorrow?" Donna admonished her son.

"Yep," the apple crunched. Gideon stood up and jogged up the stairs. "In the meantime, though, I've got an article to write!" The sentence trailed off as his younger brother disappeared down the hall upstairs and the bedroom door slammed.

"That boy needs to learn how to shut a door," Donna said, shaking her head.

"What do you think he's talking about?" Danielle asked the group?

"Oh, who knows. Gideon's got his head in the clouds all the time." Richard responded gruffly.

Mark wasn't sure though. Gideon seemed pretty hot on the trail, tracking down the truth with regards to the accusations. Was that what happened? Did Gideon uncover something to exonerate him? Is that what he meant by 'the truth shall set you free'? But what article could Gideon be talking about?

The peaceful moment had been interrupted and Mark's blood was pumping, wondering what tomorrow would bring. Mark wanted to go pound on Gideon's door and demand answers. But if he knew his brother at all; Gideon would already have headphones on and be completely in his own world. Gideon was similar to Malachi that way. Both were really smart and had no reservations about blocking out the world when they wanted to focus. If Gideon really did have an article to write before tomorrow, he'd have an energy drink open on the desk and rock music pumping through his expensive brand-named headphones.

He had to be patient. Mark sat and tried to focus on the game, but his mind was elsewhere. Donna managed to cut off his road, making hers the longest and winning the game. As they picked up the pieces, he glanced at Danielle. "Want to take a walk?"

Dani nodded. "Sure. I should get back to Aunt Maggie's soon anyway." She had changed into a pair of his athletic shorts and a T-shirt reading "Gotham City Police Department". He'd loved the dress, and even after wearing it all night, Dani was the most beautiful thing he'd ever seen. But her in his T-shirt, with the extra fabric tied in a knot at her waist, definitely held its own appeal. He grabbed a baseball hat and his shoes for himself. Then, he handed her a pair of flip flops, also far too big for her, and they headed out the door.

The night was cool; the weather today had been a blessed relief from two straight weeks of sunny days with soaring temps. The walked slowly, hand in hand, gradually covering the three blocks between his parents' house and her aunt's.

"What do you think Gideon has?" Danielle finally asked.

"I don't know. But I hope it's something that

will put an end to all this."

Danielle stopped and turned to him. "I'm so sorry I didn't stand by you, Mark."

He squeezed her hand. "Dani, it's okay. You're here now. That's what's important." They walked a bit more, and came to the front of Margaret's house. "Will I see you tomorrow?" he asked.

"Absolutely. Whatever you need." She hugged him. "I'll be at the bakery, but Aunt Maggie wasn't expecting me until Wednesday anyway, so she won't mind if I have to leave."

"Oh yeah. I forgot our flights weren't due back until Tuesday." He tipped his head to the left. "How'd you get back so soon after the wedding?"

Dani gave a low laugh. "Apparently my friend married a billionaire. And he's a romantic."

Mark raised his eyebrows and laughed. "Oh well, a billionaire. No big deal."

"Agreed. I'd much rather have a lowly schoolteacher."

He chuckled and leaned down to kiss her. "Good. I was a little worried when I saw the pictures of you dancing with Malachi."

"Don't worry. He was just talking some sense into me."

"Hmmm," Mark kissed her again. "Remind me to send him a thank-you card."

"Based on the little I know him, I don't think he'll notice if you don't." Mark tipped his head back and let out a loud laugh at her spot-on assessment of his hyper-focused brother. Malachi didn't waste brain width on what he deemed unimportant ceremony. Mark was actually surprised Mal went to the wedding at all. He must be better friends with Calvin Gates than Mark realized.

"Goodnight, Mark. I'll see you tomorrow. I'll be praying again tonight. Truth." Danielle smiled.

Mark repeated her, knowing he wouldn't be able to sleep. He'd be praying all night; echoing the same plea. "Truth."

Chapter 25

What a Tangled Web We Weave
Monday, August 3
By Gideon Dawson

Sometimes, our lies take on a life of their own. In the small regional middle school in Western Indiana, that is exactly what happened. Whose lies, you might ask? Were they the lies of Mark Dawson, beloved school teacher and pillar of the community? Lies desperate to keep his nefarious actions a secret? Or were the lies more surprising, more devious than we ever imagined?

When news broke on July 24th that Mark Dawson, a teacher at Minden-Rogers Middle School was under investigation for inappropriate contact with students, the community was floored.

Citizens on both sides of the issues came forward to voice their opinions. There was outrage that the investigation had been kept quiet for more than six weeks. Statements of support were released, asking everyone to simply wait for the conclusion before destroying an innocent man. But as details emerged, it became clear that the allegations were anything but simple. Three separate accounts of Mr. Dawson conducting himself in a shameful manner were the basis for the investigation.

When asked for comment, school principal Steve Morton responded only that, "The investigation remains incomplete" and that "Mr. Dawson will remain on administrative leave until the matter is settled." Doesn't six weeks seem like long enough? As this journalist uncovered, it was far from cut and dried. The students accusing Mr. Dawson of inappropriate conduct presented personal testimony and text messages from their teacher in which he called them pet names such as "sweetheart" and "gorgeous". Yet, after six weeks, Mr. Dawson had yet to be questioned in the investigation. His claims of innocence seemed heartfelt. Was he telling the truth? Or was the web only becoming more tangled?

When Mr. Dawson was eventually notified of his accusers' identity, he was baffled. They were his students. Nothing more. This journalist had the opportunity to sit down with all three young women claiming they were harassed by Mr. Dawson. What I found was quite different than we expected.

I heard three very similar stories. Too similar, in fact. Once pressed, the youngest girl - only twelve years old - admitted to fabricating the stories at the request of her friend. She broke down in tears when I mentioned the possibility that Mr. Dawson could face prison based on their claims. From there, the other girls also admitted they had made up the stories as a means of getting back at Mr. Dawson for what one girl referred to as "an unfair grade".

Here is what the ringleader of this crusade told me: "I never meant it to go this far, honestly". This was stated near the end of our interview, her parents sitting nearby. "I thought my parents would complain and he'd get a slap on the wrist. I told them he was upset with me for turning him down and that's why my grades were bad. But then, the investigation started and we decided to use a website that could make fake text messages." Soon, the initial white lie told to her parents turned into even more elaborate lies about his seduction techniques. She dragged her friends into it as well and created a false chain of text message for each girl.

A tangled web, indeed.

Perhaps the most eye-opening thing about this incident isn't only the human capacity for storytelling, but the very fact that we were willing to believe the very worst about someone so easily. Mark Dawson suffered a guilty verdict in the court of public opinion far before the investigation was complete. His home was vandalized; his community turned on him. As a result of giving a student the grade she deserved. Is it so hard to believe the best about people? Or are we constantly looking for the villain? Are we eager to see justice done but too impatient to wait for the judge?

As of today, three girls have agreed it is time to stand up and speak the truth about what happened with them and Mr. Dawson. That is to say, nothing at all. But the reality of how close this upstanding teacher was to losing his job, community, and freedom is something none of us should forget. Just as we should remember the other unforeseen consequence of lies such as these. For every false accusation, the stories of those who have truly been victimized lose their potency; diluted by the untruths told before.

Chapter 26

Gideon's article hit social media, with the help of a popular online news site, and spread like wildfire. Mark fielded dozens of calls from people apologizing for doubting him or claiming they were always on his side. The press conference with Morgan, Brittany, and Lydia happened at noon. With tears in their eyes, they confessed to fabricating the entire thing. They apologized to Mark.

Surprisingly, Mark wasn't angry at them. It would have been easy to be. He'd probably insist on never teaching any of the girls again, but they were girls. Barely even teenagers. They should have known better. They admitted they had known better, in fact. But they'd made a stupid decision, and it could have cost Mark everything. But it hadn't.

A conversation with Steve that morning

informed Mark the school board was already leaning toward a not-guilty decision, even before the girls' retraction. They were waiting to call Mark in for testimony, but had already determined the text messages were fake. Many of the scenarios in which the girls claimed Mark had approached them were times when Mark was on video for cafeteria duty.

There was a certain relief in the revelation he would have been found innocent either way. But having the girls admit the accusations were blatantly false and maliciously fabricated would go much further to clear his name than a simple not-guilty finding of the investigation.

After Brittany finished reading the statement they'd prepared, Mark stepped in front of the cameras on the steps of the middle school where he'd taught for so many years. "I can honestly say this has been the worst summer vacation of my life," he laughed. "I'm immeasurably grateful that these young women have decided to do the hard thing, and tell you the truth. It's a lesson I hope they never forget. As a teacher, it's my responsibility to teach students the things they will need to be successful in life. As a Social Studies teacher, I like to think that includes the government structure of ancient civilizations and the core tenets of religions around the world. But there is something far more important I try to teach each student. And that is personal responsibility. In this society, your words have great power. But, as Spiderman reminds us," he held up his Spiderman water bottle, "with great power comes great responsibility. Your words can tear someone down or build them up. They can change the world for good, or even destroy someone's future. Don't underestimate them. And don't use them lightly." He made eye-contact with the small, sorrowful girls with a nod. "As for me; I think it's time we all moved on. I'm looking forward to getting back into the classroom and getting ready for the upcoming school year. Thank you."

Reporters yelled questions, but Mark turned his back on them. He took a few steps to his right, joining his free hand with Danielle's, where it stayed until he opened the bistro door and waved her inside before him. For the first time in ten days, Mark walked down Main Street with his head held high. No baseball hat hid his identity. He was free. Cheers went up at his entrance and he spotted his family and friends. His mother rushed over and gave him a hug.

"Oh, Mark. I'm so glad it's all over."

"Me too, Mom. Me too."

Luke was there, in his dirty jeans and stained T-shirt; Charlotte in a frilly white shirt and dark jeans. Gideon stood near the back of the group, sporting thick glasses instead of his normal contacts. Mark made his way through the crowd, smiling and nodding as people tried to engage him in conversation. But there was only one conversation he needed to have at that moment. He left Danielle behind, confident she was among friends as well.

"Gideon." Mark wrapped his arms around his larger, younger brother and slapped him on the back a few times.

They parted and Gideon gave an embarrassed shrug. "It's no big deal, bro."

"I'll never be able to thank you enough."

"Thank me? Don't worry about it." Gideon's smile brightened. "I've got job offers rolling in from all over the country! Clearing an innocent man's name? It's a story everybody wants to read."

"Well, in that case, I'm really proud of you."

"Thanks, Mark. I'm just glad I could help."

Danielle came up beside him, and laid her hand on Mark's back. "In your honor, quite a gathering this is." Then, she crossed the space and gave Gideon a hug. He hugged her back loosely, wide eyes giving away his surprise. As she stepped back to Mark's side, she said, "Thanks for your article, Gideon. Not just for clearing his name," she glanced at Mark, "but for what you said about false accusations diluting the potency of the truth." She looked up at Mark's brother.

"One of the reasons I was so sure of Mark's guilt was my own need to believe the victims. Because once, a long time ago, no one believed my own similar story. And it was the worst feeling in the world."

At her admission, Mark stilled. It made so much sense. Gideon spoke softly, "I'm sorry that happened to you. And that the truth was dismissed. But I'm really glad you came back." He pulled her in for a hug again before releasing her to Mark's waiting embrace.

Mark wrapped her in his arms, grateful for the gift of her faith in him, despite her own experiences. No wonder she wanted to believe the victims initially. He kissed her hair and tightened his hold for a moment. "I'm so sorry no one believed you." Then he swallowed. "Thank you for believing me." He'd felt alone all summer, afraid what people would say if they knew about the accusations thrown at him.

Despite his growing relationship with Danielle, he hadn't been completely honest with her. Now, there was nothing holding him back. Mark meant what he said when she returned. He wanted to spend every day of the rest of his life with her, looking for satellites in the sky and arguing about Batman vs Green Arrow.

"It wouldn't be the same if you weren't here," he admitted honestly.

Danielle flashed a smile. "I'm glad I am." She glanced around the packed restaurant at the crowd there to celebrate with him. "I expected Minden to turn on you when the accusations became public."

"I did, too, actually. And some did," Mark pointed out.

"True. Is that hard for you?"

"Kind of. I'm trying to remind myself God knows my heart. And the people here, the people who love me? They represent Minden as much as those other people." He studied her. "They love you, too, you know."

Dani shook her head. "I'm not sure about that."

"It's true. You've become as much a part of this town as I have. Even if we weren't together, people would want you to stay and run the bakery with your aunt."

"That's just because they like my cupcakes."

"There is a lot to love about your cupcakes," Mark said with a laugh. "But it's more than that. You stepped up to help Margaret when she needed you. You greet every one with a smile and share your quirky humor with us. You gave Chrissy a crocheted hamburger and french fries she keeps by the cash register, for crying out loud! And you killed Todd at cornhole, which is an accomplishment that will never be forgotten. Face it, Dani. You belong to Minden as much as anyone."

She laughed at the anecdotes he brought up. It had been a crazy summer, that was sure. "Maybe you're right."

"Of course, I'm right." Mark grinned, "It's only logical." She shook her head with a chuckle at his terrible Spock impression and he pulled her tighter. "I love you, Danielle."

"I love you, too." Then, surrounded by friends and family, and free from the burden of secrets or shame; he lowered his lips to hers.

Epilogue

Danielle rolled the twenty-sided die, called a D20, and high-fived Charlotte when she saw the eighteen. Mark, acting as their game master, spoke with a smile. "Your attack is successful. You leave the guard unconscious and enter the mansion grounds."

The game continued, and it was Danielle's turn again. Mark narrated the story he had designed. "You enter the study and find The Professor asleep. You must access the safe. What do you do?"

Danielle considered her character's strengths. "I attempt to sneak past The Professor."

"Roll for stealth." Mark looked at her over the game board, a secret glance taking her back to their first encounter in the bistro. She rolled her die. One. She covered her grin with her hands, containing the laughter.

Mark threw his head back and laughed. "You roll a natural one. The Professor wakes up and notices you. What do you do?"

Danielle composed herself and took on the persona of her character and spoke in a high, squeaky voice. "Professor, it's so good to see you again. It's been a long journey; would you be a dear and get me a glass of water?"

"Charisma check?"

She rolled her die. "Thirteen."

Mark checks his notes and said in a nasally voice, "Good to see you, Angeline. I'll be right back with your water." Danielle was amazed her relatively low roll was enough to charm the professor. She'd expected to be called out as the thief she was. "He leaves you alone in the study. What do you do?"

Danielle considered her options. "I look at the bookshelves."

Mark continued narrating, "You find a secret compartment behind the bookshelf. In the secret compartment is an ornate and heavily locked chest. Inside the chest is a smaller box, wrapped in black velvet. Inside the box is a ring." During this narration, Danielle was studying her notes, trying to figure out what her next move should be, worrying the professor would return while she snooped through his things.

She looked up at the mention of treasure. Her gaze landed on Mark holding a small black velvet box, opened to reveal a stunning diamond ring. The center stone was nestled in an intricate array of twisted silver and smaller diamonds. Mark held her gaze. "I fell in love with you the moment you walked into the tavern where I was eating."

He spoke in the nasally voice of the professor, but the character voice became subtle as he continued. "I thought I'd never find someone who as perfectly matched to me as you. Will you marry me?" Then, dropping the pretense of the character entirely, he resumed his narrator role and asked the familiar question of the game, "What do you do?"

Danielle's grin grew through the speech and laughter broke through the fingers covering her mouth. She looked around the table, now understanding why Charlotte and Luke agreed to play a game clearly not in their normal activity list. "I say yes!" she squeaked out, overwhelmed. If she imagined her dream proposal, she wouldn't have come up with a more perfect scenario. It was the perfect tribute to the way their relationship started, and to the special connection they shared as best friends, not just romantic partners.

Mark stood and came around the table place the ring on her finger. Luke and Charlotte clapped and Luke let out a whistle. Charlotte stood and brushed the wrinkles out of her white capris. "So exciting!"

She hugged Danielle and then looked at Mark, "We can be done playing, right?"

Danielle laughed at her new friend. That was exactly how Liz would have responded. "I can't believe he roped you into being a part of this!"

Charlotte looked around, "What do you mean? We wouldn't miss it. Even if it meant pretending to be a fairy or whatever I was."

Mark looked over and corrected her. "Pixie."

Charlotte shrugged. "Yeah, sure. That."

Luke spoke up, "Well, I thought it was pretty cool. And we are very happy for you two." He placed a hand on Danielle's shoulder, the other on Mark's. "You guys are perfect for each other. Beyond your shared interests, you bring out the best in each other and build each other up."

Danielle and Mark looked at each other and smiled. She studied the ring now adorning her left hand. "Think I should find a new T-shirt for the wedding?" she said absently, trying to get a rise out of Charlotte.

"If you try to wear a T-shirt to your wedding, I will personally wrestle you into a wedding dress. You got that?" Charlotte's voice was elevated and she extended a polished finger in Danielle's direction.

Danielle cracked, unable to maintain her straight face. "Oh, my goodness, you should've seen your face, girl!" The group laughed, and Charlotte crossed her arms.

"I'm not kidding. No T-shirts. Or sneakers." She gave an exaggerated shudder.

Mark reached for Danielle's hand with a grin. "She can wear whatever she'd like." Then, he got a devious glint in his eye. "Oooh, Dani. What about a theme wedding?"

She picked up on his direction and quickly began to play along. "Oh, my goodness, yes! I could be Wonder Woman and you could be Superman!"

"Come on, you know I prefer Spiderman. What about Star Trek? We could put 'live long and prosper' in our vows somehow, I bet." He held up four fingers in the Vulcan salute.

Charlotte rolled her eyes at them. "Har, har, har, guys. You're not as funny as you think."

Luke jumped in, "I've heard Star Wars is a popular one? I can dress up as Chewbacca!"

"Okay, I've heard enough." Charlotte held up a hand. "I refuse to be party to this."

Danielle laughed and laid her hand on her friend's shoulder. "I promise I'll wear a real dress, Charlotte. Help me pick it out?" Her friend loved fashion and was always dressed in the latest high-end clothes.

Charlotte brightened. "Ahh, yes! I'd love to."

"Great! We'll have to pick one for you as a bridesmaid, anyway." Dani surprised herself with the comment, but realized it was exactly what she wanted. She wanted her new friends and her old friends beside her while she promised forever to Mark. She'd have to call Casey and the rest of the Knit Night girls tonight with the good news. They still needed to meet Mark. Maybe a visit to San Francisco was in order. After all, she owed Malachi a pretty big 'thank you'.

She thought about all the people they needed to share the good news with, amazed to realize how many people she was close with. She needed to tell Aunt Maggie. And Ruth would definitely be surprised at how things worked out. It all started with a phone call from her. That day, broken down in the parking lot and out of a job was one of the worst days ever, but God had promised her His plan for hope and future. And as she was once more welcomed into the arms of her fiancé, she was eager for the future God so lovingly crafted.

THE END

Note to Readers

Thank you for picking up (or downloading!) this
book. As any author can tell you, reviews are
incredibly important to our success. Please, please,
please take a minute to leave a review on
Goodreads, or your preferred book retailer!

I had a blast writing Danielle and Mark's story.
If you couldn't tell - I'm a total geek. I played too
many video games, read too many fantasy novels,
and collected and played embarrassing trading card
games that shall remained unnamed! Learning to
embrace my quirks has always been a difficult thing
for me. Far easier to have my characters do it!

I hope you enjoyed reading about Danielle and
Mark. I pray daily my books encourage you in your
faith and your struggles. I look forward to sharing

the stories of many more characters with you. My next project will be the sisters (and poor Hawthorne!) of Bloom's Farm.

You can learn more about my upcoming projects at my website: www.taragraceericson.com or by signing up for my newsletter. Just for signing up, you will get Ruth's story - Kissing in the Kitchen - for free!

If you haven't read the first book in the Main Street Minden Series, be sure to check out Falling on Main Street, Luke and Charlotte's story.

Acknowledgments

Above all, to my Creator and the great Author of Life. There has been nothing more transformative in my life than getting to know you more through Your Word.

Many, many thanks to Kentavis, for helping me step outside my comfort zone and embrace diversity head-on. Writing characters unlike yourself is the challenge and mark of a great author. Your input has been invaluable.

To Jessica, for reading this in its raw form and helping make sure it was the best story it could be. And for your endless support. I appreciate your friendship so much!

To Gabbi, for being my biggest fan and kindred spirit.

To Carol and the other ACFW MOzarks peeps - I love going on this journey with all of you!

To Stephen and Grant, I am so blessed by the feedback, wisdom, and encouragement of our little group. We are small but mighty.

To my mother - the editor. I'm so lucky to have you as a mother and cheerleader. Thanks for all you do and all you've given me. And for being the first one to buy every book. In multiples.

Thank you to all my friends and family, without whose support and encouragement, I would have given up a long time ago.

And especially, to my husband - who gives me endless grace. Your support of this adventure is what has REALLY made it possible. I love you. And to Mr. B and Little C; you fill my world with so much joy. I love watching you grow up.

About the Author

Tara Grace Ericson lives in Missouri with her husband and two sons. She studied engineering and worked as an engineer for many years before embracing her creative side to become a full-time author. Her first book, Falling on Main Street, was written mostly from airport waiting areas and bleak hotel rooms as she traveled in her position as a sales engineer. She loves cooking, crocheting, and reading books by the dozen.

Her writing partner is usually her black lab - Ruby - and a good cup of coffee or tea. Tara unashamedly watches Hallmark movies all winter long, even though they are predictable and cheesy. She loves a good "happily ever after" with an engaging love story. That's why Tara focuses on writing clean contemporary romance, with an emphasis on Christian faith and living. She wants to encourage her readers with stories of men and women who live out their faith in tough situations.